A
TOR
DOUBLE
ACTION
WESTERN

Look for Tor Double Action Westerns
Coming soon from these authors

MAX BRAND
ZANE GREY
LEWIS B. PATTEN
WAYNE D. OVERHOLSER
FRANK BONHAM
STEVE FRAZEE
WILL HENRY
CLAY FISHER
HARRY SINCLAIR DRAGO
JOHN PRESCOTT

Wayne D. Overholser

THE RIDERS OF CARNE COVE

LAST COWMAN OF LOST SQUAW VALLEY

TOR®

A TOM DOHERTY ASSOCIATES BOOK
NEW YORK

THE RIDERS OF CARNE COVE

Copyright © 1946 by Better Publications, Inc. First published in *West*.

LAST COWMAN OF LOST SQUAW VALLEY

Copyright © 1942 by Fictioneers, Inc. First published in *Ace-High Western*.

A Tor Book
Published by Tom Doherty Associates, Inc.
49 West 24th Street
New York, N.Y. 10010

Cover art by Ballestar

ISBN: 0-812-50526-3

First edition: May 1990

Printed in the United States of America

0 9 8 7 6 5 4 3 2 1

THE RIDERS
OF CARNE COVE

CHAPTER 1

Decision Day

Mack Jarvis came out of his feed store and into the street, pausing there in the spring sunlight while the restlessness in him boiled until the ferment was in his mind. It had been this way all through the months since he had quit riding for the Tomahawk outfit and had bought the feed store here in the town of Axhandle.

He never should have done it, and he had known it then as well as he knew it now. But he had set himself to do two things, one of which would make the other possible. He could have done neither if he stayed with the Tomahawk.

"Mack!" Natty Gordon called. "Lou's setting 'em up in the Casino. He wants everybody over there. Says he's got a couple of things to tell us."

The little deputy ran on along the boardwalk without waiting for Mack's answer. It was like Gordon, Mack thought, to be running errands for Lou Kyle. Too, it was like Kyle to send out word he had something to tell, and expect everybody to light out on a high lope to hear what it was. What was more, they would. All but Mack Jarvis. He could wait and hear second-hand what Kyle had to tell.

Mack slanted across the street to the Top Notch Cafe, stamped dust from his boots, and went in. "Howdy, Betty," he said, swung a long leg over a stool, and sat down. "Coffee."

"What's the matter with Natty Gordon?" Betty Grant asked, as she poured the coffee.

"He was running another one of Lou Kyle's important errands. We're all supposed to trot over to the Casino and hear somethin' Kyle's got to say."

"I didn't think Natty would hurry like that to enforce the law." Betty watched Mack spoon sugar into his coffee. "You going?"

"I ought to," Mack said sourly, "seeing as Kyle owns the bank, and the bank holds a mortgage on my store building which I can't pay. But I don't have much appetite to hear him blow off."

For a time Mack sat stirring his coffee, staring unseeingly at the pies on the shelf behind the counter. His life had been a wild stream thrown down a rough and rocky channel. It was more than a year ago that he had quit the Tomahawk and put every cent he had saved or could borrow into his feed store. He hated it. He hated everything about it. He hated the bookkeeping. He hated being inside. Still, knowing it would mean all that, he had made his choice.

He sat with his long legs bent behind him, gray eyes narrowing as he looked back along his twenty-seven years, saw the one bright spot in his life, and saw in that same glance the shadows fencing it in.

"Inky" Blair, editor of the local paper, came in and hoisted his heavy body onto a stool beside Mack. "You going over to hear what Kyle's got to say?" he asked.

"I'll read about it in the Times." Mack laid a coin on the counter. "Sometimes I wonder about that huckleberry. He's got the stage line, does all the freighting into Axhandle, owns the bank and the Mercantile, and he got 'em in a mighty short space of time."

"He didn't have so much when he came in here," Inky

said. "Anyhow, he doesn't run your feed business and he doesn't run my newspaper."

"The two independent citizens of Axhandle," Betty said. "You'd better go, Mack. Might be Kyle's going to say something about you."

"Come on, son." Inky moved toward the door.

There was something here Mack couldn't put his hands on. It wasn't like Betty to be as worried as she was, nor was Inky often deadly serious as he was now. It was as if a shadow had fallen across Mack's path, and from where he stood he could not see the substance that gave the shadow form.

"I hate to give Kyle the satisfaction of knowing I jump when he whistles," Mack said, as he reluctantly followed Inky into the street. He laid his gaze on his friend's rotund face. "You and Betty seem to know something I don't."

"So help me, son, I don't," Inky blurted. "Might be I'm boogered over nothing, but I've got a hunch this is the day you decide one way or the other."

"What are you gabbin' about?"

"You'll soon know."

Inky put a shoulder to the batwings of the Casino Saloon and went in, Mack behind him.

There were a dozen men in the place, lined along the bar. Lou Kyle was in the middle of the group, a blocky, black-eyed man driven by a great ambition that would never let him stop short of death. But in the year Mack had operated the store, he had learned that Kyle was not a man to drive hard at the thing he sought. Rather he would take any wide and circuitous route that promised the greatest success and least risk. He was doubly dangerous, Mack judged, because he was both a schemer and a killer.

An expression of malicious triumph crossed Kyle's face when he saw who had come in; triumph mingled with the shrewd cunning that was always there in his dark eyes.

"All right, gents," Kyle called loudly, his words stopping the run of talk along the bar. "Step up, and drink hearty. We're taking two rounds because I've got two important things to say."

"Spit her out, Lou!" Natty Gordon yelled. "We're right behind yuh."

Kyle grinned and motioned to the bar.

"Put her down, boys, and then bend your ears this way."

The deputy, Natty Gordon, was one of a fawning bunch of lame-brained fools who stood around like a pack of hungry hounds with their mouths open, waiting for whatever juicy morsel Lou Kyle felt like tossing them. That was the way Mack saw them.

He left his drink on the bar, a sourness washing through him. He was thinking that the only one here who could be called a man was Inky Blair.

Kyle had stepped away from the bar and stood facing the townsmen, his eyes covertly on Mack. It struck Mack, then, that what Kyle was going to say would affect him mightily. The whole play, he was thinking, was rigged for his benefit.

"I'll make the less important announcement first," Kyle said. "I've decided to go into the feed business. It will be run in connection with the Mercantile."

A dozen pairs of eyes whipped to Mack, then came back to Kyle. It was exactly what Mack should have expected. Lou Kyle was a showoff. He had taken this way of saying he was going to put Mack out of business instead of using the bank to close him out, because it gave him a chance to perform before an audience. And he would put Mack out of business, because folks would be afraid to buy from anyone else.

Kyle, Mack thought as he watched him, was like an egotistical actor determined to squeeze the last clap of applause from his audience. They were giving him what he wanted—slapping him on the back, shaking his hand, telling him loudly that he would get their business.

"This is just a starter," Kyle said, as he glowed. "Here's the real one, and I don't mind saying I'm the luckiest gent alive. I'm happy to announce my engagement to Miss Rosella Wade." Again his eyes came to rest momentarily on Mack's face. "I know I have your wishes for my happiness. That is, most of you."

* * *

There was a moment of silence, silence broken only by men's gusty breathing and the shuffle of feet, silence that left Kyle staring at the men along the bar in puzzled uncertainty. All of them knew why Mack had left the Tomahawk and bought the feed store. For a man to use his wealth and power to drive a competitor out of business was one thing; to use that power to steal the girl a man loved was something else. It was too much even for these men habitually subservient to Lou Kyle's will.

In Mack there was a shocked stillness, a vacuum of thought and feeling in which life stopped, and there was no hope. Then it passed, and he was thinking:

"He's done it this way for me. He wants me to break before everybody in town."

Coldness ruled Mack then. However deep the hurt, Lou Kyle would not see the wound. It was Mack's voice that first broke the silence. He stepped toward Kyle, lean face without expression.

"I hope Rosella will be happy. Any man who has her love is to be congratulated."

"She recognized a good man when she saw one," Kyle taunted.

There was a crescent-shaped scar on Mack's right cheek, the result of a fist fight he'd had when he had ridden for Tomahawk. In those days the solution of any problem had been easy. He cracked the easy ones with a pair of fists; the tough ones with a gun.

It was different now. The years had brought a cold and sober judgment, a self-control that kept his hands at his sides, but it was a self-control that now was near the breaking point. Mack's right hand came up to his face, finger tips rubbing the crescent-shaped scar, a signal that he was withholding his rash impulses. Inky, recognizing the sign, moved forward to stand beside Mack.

"Let's drift, son," Inky said.

"She'll sure make yuh a pretty wife!" Natty Gordon called from the bar. "When's it goin' to be?"

No one else voiced the deputy's congratulations. Mack didn't move, nor did Kyle answer Natty Gordon's question.

The banker and the former cowboy stood facing each other—tall, gray-eyed Mack Jarvis, whose love for Rosella Wade went back over the years, and thick-bodied Lou Kyle who could offer Rosella everything that money could buy.

There was silence again that ribboned on and on until it was unbearable. The men along the bar and Inky Blair, who kept his place beside Mack, could not guess what the next seconds might bring. The feeling between these two men now facing each other was not new.

The issues were as old and fundamental as life itself, and the clash between them had been predestined by a willful fate that now was working out one of the tightest knots it had ever tangled into its twine.

Again it was Mack's voice that broke the silence.

"I feel sorry for Rosella if she thinks she's getting a good man, Kyle. You're a little man, and if you were honest, you'd admit that. This business is a right fair sample. You cooked it up thinking I'd crawl out of here like a worm. You've got me wrong, mister. I ain't crawlin' out of here for any little man."

At the back end of the bar a great bear of a man shook himself, shoved the empty sarsaparilla bottle back, and plodded toward Kyle, head down. He was Tash Terris, as great of muscle as he was small of brain. He was Kyle's man, body and soul.

"You're talking like a big man," Kyle said to Mack, "which doesn't make you one."

Tash Terris was standing beside Kyle then, beady eyes honed to a sharp wickedness.

"Want I should give it to him now, Boss?" he said.

"No need for trouble," Natty Gordon called from the bar. "You hear, Lou?"

Kyle smiled, but it was a smile that held neither mirth nor pleasure. This, Mack saw, was not going the way Kyle had planned. Whether he had signaled Terris or not, Mack couldn't tell. In either case, Terris was here beside him, but still he hesitated. His eyes held the glitter of black frost. It was as if he wanted to see Mack smashed, but there was a natural caution in him that held him back.

He jerked a thumb toward the end of the bar where Terris had been standing. "Go on, Tash. Get."

Then his eyes came again to Mack, and there was disappointment in them.

"I'll carry your good wishes to Rosella," he said.

"Thanks."

Mack wheeled out of the saloon and turning toward the feed store, strode rapidly along the boardwalk, lips tightly pressed together. Inky ran beside him, his fat body shaking.

"See what I meant when I told you you'd have to decide one way or the other?" he asked between puffs.

"Yeah, I see, and I've decided. I'm goin' to skin Lou Kyle and hang his hide on perdition's outside door to dry!"

CHAPTER 2

Bullets from the Rim

Jarvis swung into his feed store and striding past "Dad" Perrod, went on to his living quarters in the back. Perrod worked for Mack at times, and made up, with Inky Blair and Betty Grant, the sum total of people in Axhandle whom Mack could call friends.

"Get my horse out of the stable, Dad," Mack called over his shoulder, and went on into the kitchen.

He was stuffing food into a flour sack when Inky came in. He looked up and grinned crookedly.

"I feel kind of like a man coming out from under that chloroform stuff when he's had a leg chopped off," he said.

"I know how you feel," Inky said. He put his fat shoulders against a door casing, wanting to say something and not finding quite the right words. "What do you reckon made Rosella tell that son of Satan she'd marry him?"

"It's her dad." Mack shrugged. "She thinks a lot of old Soogan, and he wants her hitched to a lot of dollar signs before he cashes in." He knotted a string around the grub sack and tossed it on the bed. "That's why I bought the store, and a whale of a bad deal it was, but I figured I'd make more than the thirty a month I got buckarooing for Soogan."

Mack took his gun-belt down from a peg on the wall and buckled it around him.

"Reckon I'll never be rich enough to make Soogan think I'd be a fit son-in-law," he remarked, straightening.

"I guess they're fixing to get hitched right away," Inky said sourly. "Rosella was in town a few days ago, and asked Betty to make her wedding dress."

Mack stepped into the corner and came back with his Winchester, hiding his feelings behind an expressionless mask.

"Sounds like it," was his only comment.

"I wish Betty Grant thought as much of me as she does of you," Inky said.

"Betty don't think much of me. You've been writing too many editorials—your imagination's workin' overtime."

"Maybe." Inky jabbed a forefinger at the Winchester. "You aiming to fill Kyle's hide full of holes?"

"Mebbe later. Right now I'm wondering why Kyle took a notion to go into the feed business."

"I'm guessing the railroad's the answer," Inky said. "It seems to be more than talk this time. There's several surveying outfits along the right of way south of here, and it looks as if they'll start grading any day."

"It takes a lot of horses to make a railroad grade," Mack said thoughtfully. "They got to eat."

Inky nodded. "I don't think the railroad company has made any official announcement, but a man told me yesterday he'd seen a lot of construction material piled up in Minter City."

"Kyle would know about that before anybody else around here would."

"I'm guessing that answers your question, Mack. You going out to see the Carne boys?"

"Figgered I would."

Perrod had come in. He stood in the doorway, pulling at his beard, faded eyes mirroring the worry that was in him.

"You're crazy if you ride out to the Cove," he protested. "They'll plug yuh first and talk second."

"I bought hay from 'em last year. I'll make out." Mack picked up his Winchester. "I'll be gone for a day or so, Dad. Kyle says he's going to have a crack at the feed business, and he might get rough. If you want to lock up, go ahead."

The old man flinched as if he had been struck.

"Mack, you ought to know me better'n that."

A crooked grin came to Mack's face. "Looks like I've got a friend or two."

"Yeah, for all the good they'll do." Perrod jerked a thumb at Inky. "That keg of taller won't do yuh any good, and I'm too old."

"There's Jimmy Hinton in the desert," Inky said, "but he spends too much time reading Plato and Shakespeare to be any good fighting. Son, you'd be smart to keep on riding."

"I ain't smart. So long." Mack nodded, and walked out.

He mounted his sorrel gelding, and took the high desert road out of Axhandle.

When Mack Jarvis reached the rim east of town, he reined up, and looked down upon Axhandle. It was a pleasant place, made pleasant by the rows of trim poplars, the picket fences, the white houses with green shutters. It was set alongside the swift water of Pioneer Creek where it broke out of the trench it had dug between the Sundown Mountains on the west and the high desert on the east.

Mack shifted in the saddle and stared across the valley. Held between rapidly widening walls of rimrock, Pioneer Valley was a patchwork of sagebrush and grain fields. Some day it would be cut into small, irrigated farms. That day would come when the Government dammed Pioneer Creek above Axhandle and used the high walls of the canyon for a reservoir. Then a feed store in Axhandle would be a prosperous business, but it might be five years, perhaps ten, and "Soogan" Wade had not let Rosella wait.

Mack turned his sorrel, and went on. Five miles from town he swung north, leaving the country road that would have taken him to Soogan Wade's Tomahawk, and followed the twin ruts that led to the canyon farm known as Carne Cove.

Here on the high desert, as on most of the bunchgrass

range of eastern Oregon, water was life. There was a deep well at Wade's home ranch, and a few scattered springs that were little more than seeps. Pioneer Creek flanked Tomahawk range, but only in one place did the east wall of the canyon form a gradual slope so that cattle could go down and drink.

As Mack covered the ten miles between the county road and Carne Cove, his mind went back to Rosella Wade. A great emptiness came into him, a vacuum where a dream had been. More than anything else he had wanted his own home.

Mack's parents had died when he was six. From that time his youthful years had held little that made pleasant memories. There was work and more work, and often too little to eat.

It had been a long trail south to the Border, then north to the Axhandle country in eastern Oregon, and on that trail Mack Jarvis had been a tumbleweed who had found no fence to rest against until he had signed on with Soogan Wade. Then he had met Rosella and had loved her.

The first time Mack saw Rosella the dream had come to him, tall and wide and deep. It had stayed with him through the heat and cold, the thirst and hunger, the nights without sleep and the soul-deep weariness that is a buckaroo's lot. It had stayed with him after he had bought the feed store, a year that had been like a prison sentence. Now it was gone, leaving in him that strange emptiness which comes to a man when there seems no purpose in his living.

Mack reached the Carne gate and reined up, staring at it in profound amazement. Years ago old man Carne had blasted a narrow road out of the side of the canyon that gave a steep passage to the floor of the Cove. He had blocked the entrance with a gate of light juniper poles, letting his own evil reputation keep strangers away.

The present barrier was entirely different from the old juniper gate. It was made of pine logs which the Carne boys must have brought from the Sundowns beyond Jimmy Hinton's homestead. The logs had been recently cut, for the

sawed ends had not yet been discolored by the spring rains.
One end of the gate was hinged to a heavy post; the other
end was chained and padlocked to an equally heavy post.

Tacked to the top log of the gate was a scrawled sign, the
words spelled in the Carnes' own original style:

NO INTRINSE TU NOBODE RODE DINIMITED
STA OUT

Mack swung down and walked to the gate. He put a palm
against a post, and found it as solid as it looked. This had
been no easy job, and was a senseless one as far as Mack
could see. He had never heard of anyone going into the Cove
outside of the Carnes themselves, except old Soogan Wade.
And Wade hadn't stayed long. The youngest Carne boy,
"Cat," had escorted him out with a gun.

For a time Mack stood smoking, trying vainly to think of
some logical explanation for what the Carne brothers had
done and could not. Old man Carne had homesteaded the
Cove long before there had been an Axhandle. He and his
wife had died, both without friends, and his boys had followed the same aloof pattern of living except that they did
come to town occasionally to get blind, roaring drunk.

It had been on such an occasion the summer before that
Mack had cornered the oldest boy, Dan, and arranged to buy
fifty tons of hay. The Carnes had hauled it, and there had
been no trouble, but this year Mack couldn't afford to wait
until the Carnes got thirsty.

Mack climbed to the middle log of the gate and, leaning
over it, looked down upon the Carne buildings. The log house
was set hard against the cliff almost below the gate. There
was a barn, a number of smaller buildings, and two corrals.
Three wagons with hayracks on them stood at the end of the
barn. The alfalfa fields were green, and Mack guessed the
first cutting was not far distant.

Swearing softly, Mack got down, and drew his gun. He
could shoot the padlock off, and ride down. They had no

business padlocking their gate. He stepped back, and lined his gun on the padlock—but he didn't squeeze the trigger.

A Winchester spoke from the jumble of lava to his right. The first bullet lifted his hat from his head. The second breathed by within inches of his cheek. Hard on the heels of the dying echoes of rifle fire came the flat-toned voice of Cat Carne.

"Stick that iron back in leather, Jarvis! Then mount and ride like the devil was settin' your saddle with yuh!"

The first wild impulse that rocketed across Mack Jarvis' brain was to obey—to mount and make a run for it. Then the impulse passed. He dropped his gun into leather, and slowly brought his hands above his head.

"I rode out here to talk to you boys, Cat!" he called.

For a moment there was no answer, a moment that strained Mack's nerves to the breaking point. Cat Carne was the youngest and most unpredictable of the unpredictable Carne family, a skinny, quick-tempered man with three killings to his credit that Mack knew about. It would be like him to go into a sudden rage because Mack had not obeyed his orders, and shoot him down.

But Cat Carne didn't shoot. "What you want, Jarvis?" he asked.

"Come on out, Cat. I'll bust a lung hollering at you."

Again there was silence while young Carne turned it over in his mind. Then his gaunt body rose from its hiding place in the tumbled lava mass. He came toward Mack slowly, the cocked Winchester carried hiphigh, cold green eyes not wavering from Mack's face.

When he was ten feet away, he stopped, and cuffed back his battered Stetson. His voice held a grudging admiration when he said: "You've got nerve, Jarvis. Most hombres would of lit out of here so fast they'd have left their shadder standing by the gate."

"Thanks." Mack picked up his Stetson. "Long as we're passing out compliments, I don't mind giving you one. You've got quite a name around Axhandle for being a tough hand, after you salivated that gambler last winter."

Carne's skinny face showed his pleasure.

"Aw, shucks, that wasn't anything. That jigger was plumb slow. Why, I had time to blow my nose twice before I plugged him."

"Pretty fast job, I'd say." Mack jerked his thumb at the gate. "What's the idea of that, Cat?"

Carne's green eyes narrowed. "What the Carnes do is their business, Jarvis."

"That's right," Mack agreed. "Only thing is folks will talk. I figured if I knew the reason I could put 'em straight."

"We don't want no snooping. That's all."

"Nobody ever bothered you boys, did they?"

"You're blame right we been bothered," Carne said savagely. "Old Soogan Wade come plumb down to the house just to ask about some hay."

"That reminds me, Cat. I came out here to see about buying your hay this year. Might be able to use all you've got. Figured I'd take the carry-over to boot."

"Can't let yuh have none," Carne said quickly. "We ain't even letting Soogan have none. Wouldn't surprise me none to see him come snoopin' around again, and he'll get plugged between the eyes if he does." Carne snickered. "Mebbe you'd like it if he did. I hear he won't let you marry his gal."

Mack shook his head. "I wouldn't want him beefed."

Carne snickered again. "I don't know why a man wants to have a danged female around but the Wade gal is plumb pretty for a fact. I hear she nabbed Lou Kyle. Guess you kind of got kicked in the face."

Swiftly Mack's temper was rising, but he couldn't let it go. Not yet. And he was thinking that it was queer Cat Carne would know about the engagement of Rosella and Kyle. None of the Carnes had been in town for a month. That meant, then, that Lou Kyle had been out here talking to them.

"My hard luck," Mack said casually, and then asked: "Is Kyle buying all your hay?"

Carne nodded.

"Payin' us a dollar more'n you gave us last summer."

"You reckon Kyle would let me have some?"

"No, sir. You're goin' to be plumb out because he'll sell all he can get to the railroad, and—" Cat Carne caught himself, a quick wave of red washing across his narrow face. His voice was coldly hostile when he said, "Get, Jarvis! Don't snoop around here no more, or by glory, I'll drill yuh on sight. Go on now!"

Cat Carne was ready to kill. It was there in the shrill tension in his voice, in the sudden hardening of his green eyes.

Mack Jarvis would gain nothing by staying but a bullet in his brain. He nodded.

"So long, Cat," he said quietly, and mounted. He didn't look back as he rode away.

CHAPTER 3

Visitors in the Night

Disappointment was keen in Mack Jarvis. He might have known Kyle would not give his hand away until he was certain where the big cards lay. The Jarvis Feed Store was done. Mack might as well ride back and pull down the sign. He still had a few tons of hay and some grain—that was all. And he couldn't afford to have more freighted in from The Dalles.

Inky Blair's guess as to why Kyle had gone into the feed business was confirmed by the slip Carne had made, but the knowledge, now that Mack had it, was of no great value to him. He could see little sense in seeking a market among the railroad construction camps when he had nothing to sell.

He might still be able to pick up some grain and possibly a few tons of rye hay from the dry farmers in the valley below town, but there was no real hope in him. The chances were that Kyle had been there ahead of him.

Mack made camp that night beside Buck Spring, and as he cooked supper he thought of the future of the Tomahawk range. If Soogan Wade could borrow the money to drill deep wells, the high desert could support twice the number of cattle it did now. But such developments were years ahead unless—and Mack swore bitterly at the thought—Lou Kyle had agreed to put up the money for these wells after his marriage to Rosella.

For a time Mack sat smoking beside the fire, the desert all around him, a range he had ridden many times when he had buckarooed for the Tomahawk. Now, with the sun gone from the sky, there was no motion and no sound; only a great sweep of land belonging to Soogan Wade, an empire that would go to Rosella after Soogan Wade died.

There had been a day when this high desert had been dotted with small outfits. But Wade had shoved them out of his way just as Kyle now was shoving opposition out of the way in Axhandle.

Mack built up the fire and lay on his back, head on his saddle, eyes on the clear, far brightness of the stars. The thoughts in his mind were the disturbed, bitter thoughts of a man who suddenly finds he has no anchor to hold him. He had been that way before he had met Rosella. Now there was nothing but a faint hope that a broken dream might be pieced together.

The thudding of a running horse came to Mack from somewhere north of him. He sat up and listened, and when the sound was gone, he lay back and relaxed. Likely a Tomahawk hand riding back to the ranch, he thought.

His thoughts, without conscious guidance, came again to Rosella. He forgot about the rider until, minutes later, he heard a horse coming through the junipers directly behind him.

With one quick swing of his foot, Mack scattered the fire, and spilled on over it into the sagebrush. He plucked his gun from its holster, turning back toward the still bright coals, and waited. Then relief washed through him, and he felt suddenly foolish.

"Why did you kick the fire out, Mack?" Rosella Wade's voice came from the darkness.

Mack slipped his gun back into holster, and rose.

"Guess I'm a mite boogery."

He scraped the coals together, and as he piled on more

sagebrush, Rosella rode close to the fire. When there was a flame again, he looked at her for a long moment, satisfying the deep hunger for the sight of her that had been in him.

Rosella sat motionless in the saddle, watching him closely, her hands folded over the horn. She was a tall, shapely girl who carried herself with uncommon grace. Now, coming in off the desert, dust lay in a thick gray coat upon her riding skirt and green jacket, yet she was perfectly poised, thoroughly at ease and utterly desirable.

Honey-gold hair curled under the brim of her Stetson. Her red lips held a small smile in their corners, a humor that was reflected in her blue eyes.

"This is like coming home, Mack," she said softly.

"Reckon so."

"You haven't been out to see us for a long time," she prodded.

Anger gave a sudden sharpness to Mack's words.

"Why should I? It's Lou Kyle you want to see, ain't it?"

Her lips formed the word "No," but she didn't say it. She sat a moment watching him, holding her emotions under a tight discipline. Then she said:

"You've heard."

"Kyle got us together in the Casino so he could have the proper congratulations." Then the stiffness broke in Mack and words, no longer dammed by self-control, rushed out of him. "Rosella, I know Soogan's held a dollar sign in front of your eyes ever since you've been big enough to walk, but that shouldn't have been enough to make you give Lou Kyle your promise."

Her words came to him across a great distance. "It's just possible I made up my own mind."

"I don't think so," Mack said sharply. "Soogan shoved you into Kyle's arms, and there'll be a day when he'll feel like shooting himself for it!"

"Perhaps it's just as well you haven't been out to see us," she said.

Mack gestured wearily. "I know what Lou Kyle is. Whatever you think of me, don't marry him."

He would not beg her, would not let her know what she had done to him. She should have known. He changed the subject.

"I heard your hoss going lickety-larrup, then didn't hear it, and next thing I knew you showed up right at my back."

"I was going home," she said, "but when I saw your fire, I thought I'd better see who it was. We've got trouble, Mack. I'm afraid of what will come of it. The boys are finishing the round-up, and we're short. I don't know how many but a lot."

"Short?" Mack laughed. "That's locoed talk. Soogan never had a beef stolen in his life. They couldn't be. Nowhere for 'em to go."

"That's just it. Dad says it's like having a ghost—"

A gun roared behind Mack, the bullet raising a geyser of sparks from the fire.

"Don't move!" Rosella whispered.

Slowly Mack's hands came up. He was thinking of Cat Carne, but it wasn't Carne's flat, hard voice that came to them from the junipers. It was the voice of Metolius Neele, a Tomahawk hand.

"Keep 'em up, Jarvis," Neele said. "Rosella, light out for home."

Mack would have felt better if it had been Cat Carne. The feeling between him and Neele went back to the first day he had ridden for the Tomahawk. Slowly one hand dropped to his face, fingers rubbing the crescent-shaped red scar. Neele's fist had given him that scar. But Mack had licked Neele, the only time the man had ever taken a beating, and Neele was not one to forget. He had waited a long time for this moment.

Neele rode into the firelight, a cocked Colt held unwaveringly on Mack. He was a red-haired man whose bright blue eyes were constantly alert for trouble. His thin-lipped mouth held a sly smile as if he had caught Rosella and Mack in some furtive act they had been carefully trying to conceal.

"I suppose Dad put you to playing nursemaid for me!" Rosella cried furiously.

"Somethin' like that," Neele agreed, his eyes pinned on

Mack. "You go on now, Rosella. I'll ride into town and tell Kyle about you two."

"I wouldn't do that." Mack edged away from where he had stood beside Rosella's horse. "What Kyle hears is going to be what Rosella tells him."

"You ain't in no shape to tell me what'll happen, mister." Neele jerked a thumb in the direction of the Tomahawk ranchhouse, and nodded at Rosella. "Soogan figgered you was up to somethin'."

"You haven't seen anything and I'm not up to anything!" Rosella said flatly. "I saw the light of his fire, and I thought it might be some of the rustlers, so I rode over to see."

"Rustlers!" Neele bellowed. "That's it! Sure as Tophet's hot. That's what he's out here for! Where are them cows you stole, Jarvis?"

"Got 'em in my pocket. Wouldn't be no other place to keep 'em."

"Funny, ain't you?" Neele sneered. "If you're as smart as you're comical, mebbe you cooked up a scheme to get rid of three hundred head. Or mebbe that nester friend of yours thought up something!"

"Mebbe Jimmy keeps the cows with his hogs, Metolius. Or he might have fattened his hogs on beef. Jimmy Hinton's a right smart hombre."

Neele shot a puzzled glance at Rosella as if he didn't know how to get her started, then brought his eyes again to Mack.

"Guess I'll take you into town and turn you over to Gordon."

Mack knew he would never reach town alive. He edged around the fire hoping for some kind of a break and seeing little chance for one. Sooner or later Rosella would ride on, not knowing what was in Neele's mind. Then there would be only the question of when Neele would kill him.

"You haven't got anything to hold Mack on," Rosella said scornfully.

"Either he's a cow thief, or he's here to meet Lou Kyle's girl on the sly," Neele snarled. "Either way Soogan or Kyle would say I done right if I beefed him. Jarvis, throw your saddle on your bronc!''

Rosella whirled her horse, and put him hard at Neele's mount. The action came without warning and the Tomahawk man was entirely unprepared. His horse spun, reared, and came close to piling him. When he had fought the animal back under control, he had lost his Colt and found himself looking into the black bore of Mack's gun.

''Drop your Winchester alongside that hogleg, mister, and ride,'' Mack said, his voice ominously hard.

For a moment the man hesitated, hate bright in his eyes. Then reluctantly he let his rifle go.

''You're a she-devil!'' he said to Rosella. ''Before I'm done, I'll square this with both of you.''

Then he rode away into the junipers.

''Thanks, Rosella,'' Mack said. ''My hide ain't worth much, but I'm obliged to you for keeping some holes out of it.''

''Your hide is worth a great deal, Mack,'' she said impulsively.

''If you really think so,'' he said roughly, ''why did you give your word to Lou Kyle?''

For a moment Mack thought Rosella was going to give him an answer. Then she put her horse around, keeping the back of her head to him so that he could not see her face.

''You'd better kick out your fire again,'' she called over her shoulder. ''And don't stay here in the morning!''

Then she was gone, the night and the junipers hiding her, and presently the sound of her horse's hoofs died away. There was only silence, then, save for the stamping of Mack's sorrel and the far cry of a coyote. It was a silence that stretched into the night while the fire went out, and a great loneliness was in Mack Jarvis.

CHAPTER 4

Kyle Makes an Offer

Before the starlight had died in the morning, Mack was in the saddle and riding southeast toward Pioneer Valley. He spent the morning and most of the afternoon riding from one farmhouse to another, but the answer to his question was always the same. They needed every bushel of grain and every ton of hay they had kept.

Most of them cursed their luck because they didn't have some to sell to the railroad graders. Nearly all of them seemed convinced that the long-looked-for railroad was finally on the way.

It was a bad deal fate had given him, Mack thought somberly, as he rode back to Axhandle that evening. For a year he had operated his feed store, making a poor living selling grain and hay to the Axhandle livery stable and the cowmen in the West Sundowns, hog feed to Jimmy Hinton, and odds and ends to the dry land farmers and townspeople. He had hung on because he had hoped something would happen which would give him the stake he needed. Now that the something had happened, it was too late.

Mack left his sorrel in the stable, and found Dad Perrod alone in the store.

"Any business?" he asked.

"Shore." Old Perrod drew a plug of tobacco and a knife from his pocket and sliced off a chew.

"Well?"

Perrod spat at a knot-hole in the floor and missed.

"Doggone it, Mack, since Doc pulled them last twenty-four teeth, I just can't hit my hat if I hold it under my chin."

"What business did we have while I was gone?" Mack demanded.

"Oh, I took a sack of wheat over to Miss Peterson. Mack, that danged schoolmarm sure don't have no business with chickens. She eats the pullets, raises the roosters, and wonders why in thunderation she don't get no eggs. You reckon I ought to tell her?"

"No. She'll find out for herself. That all?"

"All that amounts to anything. Lou Kyle came in this morning with that overgrown quarter-brain he calls Tash Terris and wanted to talk to you. He acted like he thought you'd gone to see Miss Rosella."

Mack grinned, wondering what Kyle would say when he heard what had happened the evening before.

"What'd he want?" he asked.

"I got the idea he wanted to buy you out." Perrod spat at the knot-hole and cursed when he missed. He wiped his mouth with the back of a hair-tufted hand. "Said he'd be over soon as you got back—and by grab, there he is now!"

Mack moved away from Perrod, and stood with his left side to the counter, right hand brushing gun butt, his lithe frame tense and ready for action.

"Howdy, Kyle," he said, and nodded.

"Howdy, Mack." Kyle stood in the doorway, his stocky figure silhouetted there, his eyes making a quick survey of the store.

"You want to buy some hay?" Mack asked. "It's going to be mighty scarce around here. Some yahoo bought all the Carne boys have and this year's crop to boot."

Kyle came in, his meaty-lipped mouth spread in a wide grin.

"I'm the gent who bought the hay, Jarvis. Reckon you had your ride for nothing."

Tash Terris had come in behind Kyle, beady eyes filled with dislike for Mack. Lou Kyle was a big man, but standing now in front of Terris, he looked less than average size.

Mack jabbed a forefinger in Terris' direction.

"Have you always got to have that gorilla with you, Kyle?"

"I like him," Kyle answered. "You heard about the railroad?"

Mack nodded. "It'll be a great thing for this country. We won't have to pay the tariff we've been paying you."

"Freight will be cheaper, of course." Kyle drew a cigar from his pocket and bit off the end. "Whether you'll be around to pay any freight is something else." He felt in his pocket for a match and, finding none, turned to Terris. "Got a match, Tash?"

"Shore, Boss." Terris produced a match and handed it to Kyle.

"I'll bet that baboon dresses you, Kyle," Mack said.

A muttered oath came from Terris. He spread his hands, heavy fingers splayed, slow anger bringing a dull red to his beefy face.

"Boss, he called me a gorilla and now he calls me a baboon," he rumbled. He clenched his fists, and spread his fingers again. "Want I should give it to him now, Boss?"

"Shut up," Kyle said sharply. "Jarvis, let's get down to business. I'll give you a fair proposition. I don't like competition. I can wait and let you starve, but I'd rather buy you out. One thousand dollars for your outfit the way she stands."

"No," Mack said briefly.

"Two thousand," Kyle said. "The only joker is that you leave the country as soon as you're paid. I don't want you around here starting another store with my money."

"No," Mack said again. "I don't get it, Kyle. It don't make sense for a nickel-pincher like you to talk about two thousand dollars when you claim all you've got to do is to set and starve me out.''

''I told you I didn't like competition, but if that's the way you want it, I'll get rid of you in one way or another. Make no mistake about that. Come on, Tash.''

Kyle went out, a cloud of cigar smoke fouling the air behind him, Terris at his heels.

''Dad,'' Mack said somberly when they were gone, ''I'm crazy. I should have taken that offer.''

Perrod took another shot at the knot-hole and cackled loudly.

''I just hit the target. Guess I'll have to move back three feet. Gettin' too easy from here.''

''I said I was crazy,'' Mack repeated. ''A smart man would have taken that offer.''

Perrod sobered. ''Sure you're crazy, son, but if it wasn't for crazy jiggers like you, it would be an easy world for fellers like Lou Kyle.''

Mack walked to the front door. Evening shadows were falling across the street as the day's warmth was blown away by a cold north wind riffling in from the Sundowns. Mack rolled a smoke, wondering what there was in some men that made them stubborn, while others were as easily bent as a wheat straw in a gale. There were no tangible ties here in Axhandle to hold him. His store was a failure. Rosella would marry Kyle.

Yet now as he gave it thought, he knew there were friendship bonds holding him here, bonds that were far stronger than any money could forge. Jimmy Hinton would need help. Soogan Wade would keep pressing the homesteader until Jimmy might have to go. Inky Blair would eventually come to the place where he would take a stand against Kyle, and he would need help. Dad Perrod was too old to do a real day's work. And Betty Grant! Mack smiled a little when he thought of her, for the thought was a pleasant one. Of all his friends, she was the only one who would be able to stand on her own two feet.

It was then that Mack saw the cavalcade which turned into

Main Street from the high desert road. A buckboard was in front, with Soogan Wade driving and Rosella sitting beside him. Flanking the buckboard were two buckaroos, and behind it the full string of Tomahawk riders—all but Metolius Neele.

A hard-bitten, salty crew, these Tomahawk hands. Only Metolius Neele was Mack's enemy, but on the other hand he had no friends among them. They saw him as a close friend of a nester, and for that reason he received indirectly some of the dislike they held for Jimmy Hinton.

The buckboard wheeled past the feed store, Soogan looking straight ahead and being careful not to see him. Rosella nodded and smiled, and Mack took a wicked enjoyment in hoping that Lou Kyle was watching. Some of the buckaroos pinned stony eyes upon him, but most of them kept their gaze on the street ahead in the arrogant fashion that befitted men who rode for the biggest outfit in the country.

Mack rolled a smoke and stood motionless for a time while Rosella and her father went into the hotel and the Tomahawk men disappeared into the Casino. Suddenly he made a decision.

"Dad, watch things!" he called.

He left the store and turned into the hotel. He took a seat in the corner of the lobby and threw his cigarette violently into a spittoon. There was no satisfaction in it. There was no satisfaction in anything unless it might be in pounding some sense into Soogan Wade's head, a miracle Mack had little hope of accomplishing.

Mack saw Wade come down the stairs, moving slowly as one who is tired and puzzled and suddenly feels the weight of time. He was a medium tall man whose wrinkled face was burned to a saddle-leather brown, and there was a mildly comical look about him that came from the huge, untrimmed mustache, a look which was totally deceptive, for Soogan Wade was anything but comical. His eyes were the real index of his character. They were bright and sharp, reflecting the aggressiveness that was so much a part of him.

Wade was not an old man as judged by measures of time, but he had done three men's work back in the lean years, and the hardships of those years had sapped much of the great, natural vitality from him. Now that he had achieved success, he wanted everybody to know the distance he had come, and it was that desire to flaunt his wealth which prompted him to substitute gold coins for buttons on his coat.

Mack rose, and stepped in front of Wade.

"Funny what a man thinks he can do when he's riding high and handsome," he said.

"Get out of my way," the old cowman said darkly.

"You can shove your tally book back into your desk," Mack went on, as if he hadn't heard, "and it'll stay there, but cuss it, Soogan, you can't treat people that way!"

"I said to get out of my way!" Wade rasped. "I'm looking for Natty Gordon."

"You're going to listen if I have to rope and tie you. Kyle says he's going to marry Rosella. Soogan, if you had half the sense about men you've got about cows, you'd know Kyle wouldn't make a fitting husband for anybody you love."

"You're jealous!" Wade said truculently.

"There's only two things in life that mean anything to you," Mack went on relentlessly. "Money and Rosella. You figger if you got 'em together, you'd have everything fixed. If you had the sense of a boiled sage hen, you'd know better."

Wade's face reddened under the pressure of his rising anger.

"You ain't nothing but a puncher who thinks he's a business man! Don't try telling me my business!"

"All right." Mack gestured wearily. "I'm a puncher. I ought to be out forkin' my sorrel and listening to some cows bawl. That ain't important. I happen to love Rosella, and I want to see her happy."

"I've fixed Rosella's happiness," the girl's father snapped. "She's marryin' the richest man in Axhandle! He'll be richer, too. Lou don't miss a bet.

"He don't, for a fact," Mack agreed sourly.

"You're worth thirty a month and beans and nothin' more, Mack. I figger you're just growling because you lost your girl. If you've got any proof that Lou's a coyote who ain't fittin' to marry Rosella, I'll listen!"

Mack could make no answer that would satisfy Wade, nor could he put his fingers on an actual crime that Lou Kyle had committed. His feeling came from an accumulation of little things. He had known Kyle to close out dry farmers and small ranchers because his bank gave him the opportunity to do so. Not once had he ever heard of Kyle contributing a cent to any cause that didn't make him a profit. He interpreted every situation he met in terms of how it would affect him.

It was this ever-scheming selfishness about Kyle that told Mack he was not the man to give Rosella happiness, but it would not be a sound argument to Soogan Wade. So he only said:

"A man can't buy a woman's love."

Wade snorted contemptuously. "Money will go a blame long ways toward it, son. I don't hold to this mush and tush about love. Lou will build her the finest house in town. She'll have all the dresses she wants with lacy doodads on 'em, and she'll mix with the top crust of the country. She'll go to Portland, Frisco, Chicago. Heck, she'll go to Yurrup. You can't buy her that kind of foofaraw, and you never will."

"A woman wants something besides foofaraw."

"You ain't no expert on females," Wade said sharply. "Now I'm goin' to find Natty Gordon."

Mack stepped away then and let Wade go. Nothing could change the old man's mind about Lou Kyle. The bitterness of failure was in Mack as he stepped into the street. He had done all he could.

"Mack!" Inky Blair called. He came in a slow lumbering run from the feed store. When he was closer, he panted, "Old Soogan's lost a lot of beef, Mack. The Tomahawk boys are down in the Casino talking about it. They're claiming Jimmy Hinton done it, and they're fixing to swing him from a juniper limb!"

It had come then, Mack thought. He would have to side with Hinton—and maybe get himself hung for his trouble.

CHAPTER 5

A Rope for Jimmy Hinton

Natty Gordon centered the line of men along the bar in the Casino, with Soogan Wade on one side of him, and George Queen, the Tomahawk ramrod, on the other. The deputy was a small, carefully dressed man who posed as the law in Axhandle. He held his job because he made it a cardinal principle never to cross important men like Lou Kyle and Soogan Wade.

Now Gordon was pulling at his mustache, looking from Queen to Wade and back to Queen. He was worried and he was scared, and as Mack came up to the bar he felt a contemptuous pity for the man.

"I don't know what to do," Gordon was saying, his voice high and close to cracking. "I don't know where to begin!"

"You can ride," Wade said belligerently. "Three hundred head of beef don't dig a hole and jump into it. Likewise they don't fly off."

Gordon licked his lips nervously, then saw Mack.

"You know that country," he said. "What do you think happened?"

"I haven't got the story." Mack hooked his thumbs into

his belt and watched Wade closely. "I reckon Soogan could lose three hundred head without getting hurt."

"We ain't going to lose anything," Queen said darkly.

He was a rail of a man, all bone and hide, the fat burned out of him by long hours under a hot sun. His eyes were hard and black, his mouth a thin slash across his face. He was tough and he was proud, and his pride had been hurt. In the years he had rodded the Tomahawk, there had been no great loss of cattle. There was a big loss now, and Queen was the kind who would hang a man for it. He might be wrong, but hang a man he would.

"It ain't a question of what I can afford," Wade said coldly. "The point is that if three hundred head can disappear into thin air, so can three thousand, and we can be cleaned."

"We ain't goin' to lose anything," Queen repeated, black eyes pinned on Mack. "The answer's so plain you're all overlooking it. Jimmy Hinton's squatting on our range, and he's a good friend of yours, Jarvis. Between you, you got away with them cows, and I'm aiming to find out how."

There was stunned silence for a moment. Natty Gordon's mouth fell open in quick surprise. Wade's wrinkled face showed amazement.

Mack smiled thinly, his eyes locked with Queen's.

"I've been called a lot of things," he said softly. A finger came to his face to touch the crescent-shaped scar. "Some things a man has to take, and some he don't. Being called a cow thief is one I don't take." His hand came down. "Start smoking your iron, George."

"No trouble, boys!" Gordon squealed.

"Get down off your high hoss, George!" Wade bellowed. "You ain't swappin' no lead with Mack. You hear me, George?"

Slowly Queen straightened, hand falling away from his gun. He shot a glance at Wade.

"All right," he said hoarsely. "Let's forget it, Mack."

Mack nodded, and looked at Wade. "Soogan, losing three hundred head on Tomahawk range is the craziest thing I ever heard of. You must have missed 'em setting behind some juniper.''

"We didn't miss 'em," Wade said flatly. "We made a clean ride. I tell you they're gone!"

"Where would an outfit take 'em? North mebbe?"

Wade frowned. "Reckon not. There ain't no water in them East Sundowns. It's too long a drive to get 'em to water, and the country's too rough. Likewise they couldn't go east for the same reason."

"Mebbe they went west," Gordon jeered. "Flew across Pioneer Canyon."

"That's for you to find out," Wade snapped. "I know they didn't go south. Too many people living down there. They'd have been seen."

"I say Hinton is the one," Queen grated. "There ain't nobody else, and any critter who'd steal a spring and turn it into a hog waller would steal cows."

"Use your noggin, George," Mack said contemptuously. "You just heard Soogan say they couldn't go north, south, east, or west. That just about takes care of all directions but up and down."

"He's right there against the foothills of the Sundowns," Queen said doggedly. "Mebbe he found a spring back in them mountains."

"Soogan said you hadn't found any tracks," Mack objected.

"Lava all around Round Butte. Cows wouldn't leave tracks in that stuff."

"He couldn't take 'em on through."

"The railroad's coming in," Queen said, "and that'd give him his market."

Mack laid his gaze on Wade's face. "Soogan," he said, "you've never liked Jimmy because he's the only nester who ever had the nerve to stick on Tomahawk range after you threatened him and shot at him."

"He's got nerve," Wade admitted grudgingly, "but I'll get him off."

"Might be you dreamed up this cow-stealing yarn just to give you an excuse to pour it on Jimmy."

"No!" Wade roared. "I ain't that ornery."

There was a ring of sincerity in the old man's voice that told Mack he had made the wrong guess. He pinned his gaze on the deputy.

"Natty, there was some talk about the juniper back of Jimmy's cabin bearing fruit."

The scared look was on Gordon's face again.

"George," he said quickly, "you wouldn't let your boys do that, would you?"

Queen's grin was quick and wicked. "I can't promise what my boys would do some dark night, but Hinton would sure be smart to vamoose."

"If you swing Jimmy," Mack said slowly and deliberately, "I'm coming after you." He turned back to Wade. "Why couldn't the Carne boys have done the job?"

"Because their gate ain't far from our watering place," Wade said quickly. "If they'd been the ones, some of the boys would have seen 'em. Besides, the dirt's 'dobe there, and it'd sure hold tracks in the spring when it's wet."

Mack nodded and, wheeling away, walked rapidly toward the feed store, Inky Blair in a heavy-footed run beside him.

"Every time I try to keep up with you," Inky complained, "I lose my breath, and it takes me a week to find it."

"Get some hounds and track it. It's stout enough to track." Mack turned into the store. "Dad, saddle a hoss for me. Better let me have your roan. My sorrel's a mite tuckered."

"I'll get him," Perrod said and shuffled out.

Mack picked up his Winchester and cut across the street to the Top Notch Café. He leaned his rifle against the counter and sat down. Betty Grant watched him, smiling a little, and hiding behind that smile the knowledge she had of him.

"Steak and onions," Mack said, "and make it quick. I've got riding to do."

Inky came in. "Hod dang it, feller, you sure keep on the move. Betty, toss a steak on for me." He jabbed a fat finger at Mack. "He's going hunting again."

"What is it this time?" Betty asked.

"Coyotes," Mack answered laconically.

Mack ate rapidly, as if time was rushing away from him and there was too little of it. These two who knew him well said nothing, but when he was done, and Betty had filled his cup again with coffee, she said:

"Let me go with you, Mack. I was raised with a Colt in my hand in Piute country."

"Thanks, Betty, but I'd do less worrying if you stay here . . . Inky, tell Dad to keep an eye on things."

Mack picked up his Winchester and stepped to the door. He glanced back at Betty, thinking of her offer, and thinking, too, it was an offer Rosella would never have made. Then he went out, mounted, and rode away.

It was dusk when Mack reached the rim above Axhandle. He rested the roan, staring down at the scattered lights coming to life in the little town, then he turned his horse eastward along the country road. Worry set up strife within him. Knowing George Queen as he did, he was certain that the danger threatening Jimmy Hinton was real and imminent.

Full darkness came before Mack reached the road that turned north to Carne Cove. The last of the day had gone, and in its place were stars and a full moon. It was a strange and awesome world by night, a vast and endless expanse of sage and bunchgrass and junipers.

Mack rode steadily north, the land tilting upward as he came closer to the Sundowns. He passed the log gate barring the road into the Cove, wondered idly if Cat Carne stood guard by night as well as by day, and kept on. The smooth, cone shape of Round Butte appeared, and he was in the lava.

"Round Butte blew its head off perhaps two centuries ago," Jimmy Hinton once had said. "Practically yesterday."

"Yesterday?" Mack had laughed. "How would you figger a week, Jimmy?"

"Geologically speaking, two centuries ago is a mere nothing." Jimmy had paused then, his eyes twinkling. "You're a man of action, Mack, and there is no part of a scientist in you. What I'm trying to say is that we aren't very important.

I mean in the long pull. We think we're important because we're so close to the things that are happening. It's because we don't have any perspective.''

Mack was thinking about that conversation now as the roan made his way over a lava upthrust and came down to the flat, sand-topped earth beyond it. He was going to ask Jimmy to come to town and move in with him and Dad Perrod.

He wanted, too, a look at the dry Sundowns beyond Jimmy's cabin. It was an impossible hiding place for cattle, but it was the only one.

In the back of his mind, Mack admitted grudgingly, was the truth of Wade's statement that he was a puncher worth his thirty a month and beans and nothing more. It would be worth a try to prove the old man wrong, and it would be worth a great deal more to prove to Wade that he was wrong about Lou Kyle.

An idea came to Mack then, an idea that shocked him. Perhaps it was Lou Kyle's smart, scheming brain that was behind the cattle theft!

Immediately Mack put the notion out of his mind. It was fantastic that a man in Kyle's position would steal three hundred head of beef.

CHAPTER 6

Riders of the Night

Ahead of Mack Jarvis a light in the window of Jimmy Hinton's cabin was shining like a small, earth-bound star. Mack was surprised to see it. It was in the early hours of the morning, and he had not expected to find Hinton still up.

He rode directly to the cabin, passing alongside another twisted pile of lava looming ghostlike beside the trail. He reined up.

"Hello, the house!" he called.

Mack waited, drawing his gun and holding it ready. The door swung open. A flood of lamplight washed out and Jimmy Hinton stood there, his lank body a high silhouette in the rectangular frame.

"You make a target as big as a horse!" Mack called sharply. "Don't you know that's no way to come out of a house, you lame-brained fool?"

"Sounds like my tough friend by name of Mack Jarvis." Hinton crossed the yard. "Step down and come in."

Mack dismounted, still feeling the prod of gusty anger.

"Look, Jimmy," he said earnestly. "You're squatting on Tomahawk range. George Queen and his boys are right salty hombres. One of these days they'll call to you like I did, you'll open the door and stand there like you was the queen of the May, and blooie!''

"Shooting a man is a bad practise," Hinton said distastefully. "Causes a lot of leaks.''

"You idiot!" Mack groaned. "You crazy idiot!''

"Now that you're done belittling my intelligence," Hinton said amiably, "let's put your animal away. Then I'll brew a pot of coffee.''

After Mack's roan had been stabled and fed and Hinton was shutting the barn door, the flat echoing sound of a gunshot rode the night air to them. Then another and a third, and that was all. The silence of the high desert was around them again. There was the faint whisper of wind through the junipers. The screech of an owl and the faint cry of a coyote from some rim in the Sundowns came to them.

For full five minutes neither man moved.

"I've never heard a gunshot at night during all the months I've lived here," Hinton said then. "There's nobody closer than the Carne brothers or possibly a passing Tomahawk rider. What do you think it means?''

"Trouble for you," Mack Jarvis said grimly.

"That so?" Hinton asked carelessly. "Well, I guess we all need a little spice in our living.''

In the house Hinton stoked up his fire and started the coffee.

"What is this trouble you were talking about?'' he asked.

"George Queen allows you got away with three hundred head of Tomahawk beef.''

Hinton laughed, and reached for his pipe and tobacco can.

"Where does he think I'd put three hundred head of cattle?''

Hinton sat puffing on his pipe while Mack told him what had happened. He was older than Mack, a man with thin, sandy hair, round shoulders, and gray eyes that were bloodshot from hours of night reading. He was a strange man to pit himself against the raw life of a homestead, and yet some-

how he had made the transition from a city existence speed-
ily, and with little discomfort.

When Mack finished talking, Hinton rose and poured the
coffee.

"Interesting and crazy," he said drily, "to think I could
steal three hundred cows."

"Jimmy, it just ain't in the cards for you to stay here and
buck the Tomahawk!" Mack pleaded. "Soogan's always been
able to get rid of nesters, and he'll get you if you stay. How
about moving into town and living with me and Dad Perrod
for a while?"

"Thanks, Mack," Hinton said, a little gruffly. "You and
Dad are proof that a few decent people still survive. Not
many of the breed left, but a few."

"You're so danged smart you're a fool!" Mack said hotly.
"If you lived to be a thousand, you'd never understand men
like Metolius Neele and George Queen. If you stay here
they'll hang you higher'n Haman whether you ever stole a
cow or not!"

Hinton shrugged. "Let them come. . . . Let's talk about
something pleasant—like you and the beautiful Rosella."

"It isn't very pleasant, Jimmy," Mack said gloomily.
"She's marrying Lou Kyle."

Hinton stared at Mack in surprise.

"I'm sorry," he said. "I wouldn't have mentioned it if I'd
known." He began pacing the floor, pain deepening the lines
in his face. "A woman did that to me, Mack. She was beautiful, like Rosella." He gestured wearily. "That's why I don't
care what happens. Mack, don't let her do that to you."

A one-sided grin came to Mack's lips. "I don't aim to,
Jimmy. There's several things I want to do, like whittling Lou
Kyle down a notch or so."

There was something else that Mack wanted to do, and after
he was in bed he thought about it, but saw no way of accomplishing it. He wanted to save Jimmy Hinton's life, and he
couldn't do that if Hinton insisted on staying here. Mack had
no weapon with which to combat human indifference. He was

a spectator watching fate twist a hideous, cruel pattern, and finding himself without power to influence the shaping of that pattern. . . .

The throb of talk woke Mack from a deep well of sleep. Hinton's bunk was empty. Mack heard the snap of burning wood in the stove, and he wished dully that whoever was talking would go away. He wasn't done sleeping. Weariness from the long night ride was still in him, and he had more riding to do in the Sundowns.

The thought came to Mack's sleep-fogged brain that Hinton was talking to his hogs. Of all the fool things to do! Get up at daybreak to talk to a bunch of hogs. Then it occurred to Mack that one of the voices wasn't Hinton's, and it wouldn't be a hog talking back.

Then another voice, strident and cruel, swept the last cobwebs of sleep from Mack's brain.

"Throw out a loop, Metolius!" it said. "We're goin' to stop this cow stealin', and do it permanent. That limb on the north side of the juniper will do."

It was George Queen's voice. Mack had heard it too often to be mistaken. He leaped from the bunk and ran to a window. Hinton stood halfway between the barn and the cabin, his hands in the air, his long-jawed face without expression. A half dozen Tomahawk riders sat their saddles in front of him, naked guns in their hands. Back of Queen was a horse with the still form of a buckaroo tied face down across his saddle.

Metolius Neele was building a loop, a cruel, satisfied grin on his lips.

"All set, George!" he said. "Let's get it over with."

Mack, clad only in his underwear, grabbed up his Winchester from the corner and shoved the door open.

"George," he called, "I shoot purty well with this blowpipe! Want to see?"

George Queen couldn't have looked more surprised if Round Butte had spewed a hot rock out of its crater. He laughed, a high cackle that held little humor. "You shore look funny in them drawers, Mack," he said.

"I don't reckon I look any funnier than you did when you first saw me," Mack shot back at him. "You boys were sure taking chances riding in and getting the drop on Jimmy. You're a bunch of ring-tailed wowsers, now, ain't you?"

Mack's tone had the slashing force of a blacksnake cutting Queen across the face. Every Tomahawk man, from Queen on around to Metolius Neele, looked ashamed. None of them spoke, for there was a quality in Mack's face that told them the first one to make a hostile move would die.

Suddenly Hinton laughed. It was a soft, contemptuous sound. He moved toward Mack.

"You must have put salt on their tails, Mack," he said. "You tamed six murder-talking men in about ten seconds."

Mack didn't take his eyes from Queen. Metolius Neele was the toughest man in the bunch, but it would be Queen who would make the decision to fight and die, or live to fight again.

"I figure I've got hold of the jerk line, gents," Mack said. "If any of yuh think different, start smoking."

Still they didn't move and they didn't speak. Five of them were watching Queen, and Queen was watching Mack. The ramrod couldn't make up his mind. He had backed water the afternoon before in the Casino, and it wasn't in him to do it again.

The silence was stretching every man's nerves to the breaking point. It could not go on. Mack sensed it, and knew no real gain could come from a fight.

"Drop your irons, gents," he said. "I ain't going to stand here and argue all morning."

They let their Colts go, relief showing in their faces as they relaxed from the tension that had gripped them. Queen jerked a thumb at the dead man.

"That's Curly Usher, Mack. We found him the other side of Round Butte."

"Why were you after Jimmy?" demanded Mack.

Queen took a thin book from his pocket.

"We found this about ten feet from Curly's body," he said,

"and it's got Hinton's name on it. The killing son that got Curly was up close when he done it."

"Any sign?"

"Nothin' but this book." Queen glanced at the name. " 'Macbeth,' it says. I don't know who this Macbeth hombre is, but it's a cinch he didn't walk over by himself."

"Jimmy didn't do it, George. He can't shoot worth a hoot, even up close. Besides, Curly would have been suspicious of Jimmy, and he wouldn't have let him get close. In the third place, Jimmy wouldn't be reading that book in the moonlight."

Queen cuffed back his Stetson and scratched his head.

"Some of that makes sense," he admitted. "Soogan sent Curly and Metolius up here to the north range to keep an eye on things, and Metolius told Curly to stay clear of Hinton. We figgered he'd give himself away if we watched him."

"Metolius, were you around the Butte last night?"

"I was over at the lava field," Neele answered sullenly.

"You heard the shooting?"

"Yeah, but when I got there, Curly was dead."

Mack swung back to face Queen.

"How did you and the rest of your bunch get here so quick?"

"Soogan sent us out. He got to thinking Metolius and Curly wasn't enough. Now mebbe you know somethin' about this, Mack."

"I know Jimmy didn't do it. I got here about two o'clock. We had just put my horse away when we heard the shooting."

"I reckon you're lying to cover up," Queen said sharply. "How'd your book get out there, nester?"

"I had some things stolen several days ago," Hinton answered. "It was early in the morning. Just about this time. I was going into the pig pen when somebody hit me on the head."

"What did they take?" Queen asked.

"My knife, a pipe I've smoked for years, and that copy of 'Macbeth.' "

"That yarn is just loco enough to be true," Queen mused.

"Mebbe somebody else wants Jimmy off this range," Mack suggested.

"Yeah," Queen agreed somberly. "You goin' to let us ride?"

"Have I got your word you won't be back after Jimmy?"

"We won't unless we hit onto somethin' more'n we've got now."

"All right." Mack lowered his Winchester. "Pick up your hardware and vamoose."

Metolius Neele stepped down and handed the six-guns to the mounted men. Then, as he holstered his own Colt, he wheeled to face Mack, his eyes bright and wicked.

"I ain't never forgot what you done to me, Jarvis! There's them that figures your carcass is worth one thousand dollars. I aim to collect that dinero!"

"Any time," Mack murmured.

Neele mounted, reined in behind Queen and the six of them rode away, the last rider leading the dead man's horse.

"I guess I'm not as ready to die as I thought I was." Hinton ran a shaking hand over his face. "If you hadn't been here they'd have hanged me."

"They were fixin' to do it," Mack agreed. "Now I'm going to put my pants on before I freeze complete."

CHAPTER 7

Stubborn Homesteader

While Mack and Hinton were eating breakfast, Hinton was deeply and soberly thoughtful.

"Being accused of cattle stealing is more than I can stand," he finally said. "They don't really think I stole those cattle, do they?"

"Probably not." Mack shrugged. "Hanging somebody would make Queen feel better, and he could tell Soogan he's got everything fixed."

Hinton reached for the bacon.

"Mack," he said, "it may be presumptuous of me to offer any explanations to you since you know the country and the people better than I ever will, but it occurs to me that I'll never be cleared until the crime is solved. When we analyze the situation, we can immediately discount the supernatural. We know that I didn't do it. That leaves three possibilities. Perhaps some of the Tomahawk men stole the cattle themselves."

"No." Mack shook his head. "They're a salty bunch of boys, but they wouldn't steal. Metolius mebbe, but not the rest of 'em."

"The second possibility is that it's a lie from the start, told for the purpose of getting me off their range."

"No." Mack shook his head again. "Soogan wouldn't lie."

"All right. Number Three. The way Soogan put it, the only direction they could go would be up or down. Cows couldn't go up, but they could go down. I believe that the Carne boys stole them and then hid them in the Cove."

"Soogan figures some of his boys would have seen 'em chouse the cows through the gate."

"There might be another way known only to the Carnes," Hinton said doggedly.

"Look, Jimmy! The east side of the Cove is a straight drop down. Besides, the northern part of the rim has got a lava flow along it that makes a wall ten feet high or better. And supposing the Carnes did get the cows down there? Why wouldn't we see 'em from the rim?"

"I don't know," Hinton admitted, "but everything has a logical explanation, and I'll find it if Queen and his bunch don't hang me first."

Mack rose and reached for his Stetson.

"Funny thing about the Tomahawk boys. They'd take a herd to perdition, and if there wasn't no market there, they'd fetch 'em back, and sell 'em somewheres else."

"Then when something doesn't suit them, they become killers," said Hinton. "Strange about people, Mack. Goodness and badness is always a matter of relative thinking."

Mack stood by the door, a frown furrowing his forehead.

"You think too much, Jimmy. I don't have that trouble. I know what I'm going to do."

"You just think you do, Mack. Suppose Rosella decided she'd rather have you than Kyle. What would you do?"

"Why, I'd marry her," Mack said quickly. "I'm not a complete fool."

"You'd be a fool if you married her after she broke her promise to you. Mack, do you think you ever really loved Rosella?"

"Think?" Mack exploded. "Why, I know!"

Hinton filled his pipe, and touched a match flame to it. He watched Mack through the smoke as if turning something over in his mind that he wasn't sure should be said. Then he blew out the match, his decision made.

"Mack," he said, "because you were an orphan, you've envied people all your life who had homes and families. Isn't your loving Rosella a case of finding a girl who was pretty and desirable, and one you could fit into the dreams you'd held all through the years?"

"No," Mack said roughly. "She's mine. She belongs to me. It's just that Soogan—"

He paused then, seeing the weakness of what he was saying. Whatever pressure Soogan had put upon her, the decision had been hers.

"Get out of the country, Mack," Hinton urged. "Forget her. She's fickle and she'd give you nothing but heartaches all your life if you married her. You'd only have half her heart. She's chosen money, so let her have it."

Black fury was in Mack Jarvis then. He took a step toward Hinton, a great fist balled, a fierce desire in him to smash back into Jimmy Hinton the words he had spoken. Hinton did not back away. He stood beside the table, eyes blinking at Mack through his thick glasses, fear not a part of him.

Mack's fist fell to his side. He wheeled out of the cabin, and strode to the barn. Hinton followed and stood watching in silence while Mack saddled the roan.

"If I have offended you, Mack," he said somberly, "I can only offer apologies. There was a moment when I was alive again. It seemed to me I was living through you and being able to do the things I should have done and never had the courage to do."

"It's all right, Jimmy." A smile touched Mack's lips, the fury dead in him. "I'm going back into the Sundowns. I'll be back in mebbe a week."

"It's dry traveling. I've found two small springs. One's just above the rim about five miles from here. The other one's on the north side of Bull Mountain."

"I'll find 'em."

Mack nodded and turned his roan toward the mountains.

Mack Jarvis rode until evening, going deeper into the Sun-downs than he ever had before. It was a wild and useless country of deep canyons, rimrock and thickets of jackpine, and before the day was half gone, he was more firmly convinced than ever that it would have been impossible for any cattle thieves to have driven a herd through such a country.

Once Mack came to Pioneer Canyon and let his horse stand for a time on the rim. Directly below him was the sparkling turbulence of the creek, three hundred feet from where he sat his saddle.

Across the canyon the Sundowns were far less rugged than this spur on the east side of the creek. There was water, a good stand of merchantable timber, and large meadows of lush grass. A dozen small cattle outfits were scattered between Axhandle and the summit, and it was the untapped riches of that section which had lured the railroad up Pioneer Creek.

Mack turned his roan north. Near evening he killed a buck, dressed it, and found the spring on Bull Mountain. He made camp and after supper sat by the fire, thinking of what Hinton had said about Rosella, and feeling a sour shame for the anger Hinton's words had raised in him.

Twilight came, and night, and the stars made a bright shining over him. He was almost asleep when he heard stealthy steps moving through the jackpines. He slid away from the low-burning fire, pausing in the black shadow of a high boulder. Drawing his gun, he hunkered there motionless. For a time there was no sound.

The moon rose, throwing the jackpines into sharp relief. Mack thought first of Metolius Neele who might have followed him, of Cat Carne, and then of Lou Kyle and his creature, Tash Terris. His thoughts came back to Neele, of his saying somebody wanted Mack's death enough to pay one thousand dollars for it.

Mack heard the steps again, and tensed, finger tight against the trigger. Then the tension left him, for the man who had come into the firelight was Natty Gordon.

48 WAYNE D. OVERHOLSER

"You're one fine lawman," Mack said sharply, "coming up on a man that way."

"I won't argue." Gordon stood with his hands to the fire. "What you doin' here?"

"Trying to find them cows Queen said Jimmy had back here."

Mack threw wood on the fire and looked at the deputy in the light of the quick blaze. Dust and weariness laid a shadow over the man. He built a smoke, shoulders hunched forward, an unhappy little man who held no hope of finding the cattle for which he searched.

"A plumb mean, ornery country," he complained. "I'll bet my bottom dollar there ain't a cow this side of Hinton's homestead."

"I don't think so, either," Mack agreed, "but I'm going to look it over. Then I'm going back and stuff George's lie down his throat."

"Mind if I camp here tonight?" asked the deputy.

"Lots of room. I suppose you thought you'd found the cow thieves when you saw my fire."

"I was scared I had." Gordon got up. "Don't be too sure about Hinton, Mack. I'm going to keep my eyes on him."

"He'll sure be worried. Mebbe them cows did grow wings, Natty, and flew across Pioneer Canyon. That's what you'd better look for. An old pile of cow wings. You know how white-faces are. They always lose their wings in the spring."

"I'll watch for 'em," Gordon said drily.

Natty Gordon left the next morning, growling that there wasn't any sense of his getting saddle blisters traipsing over the country when the whole Tomahawk crew couldn't find three hundred cows.

Mack stayed in the Sundowns for a week. Then, satisfied that Soogan Wade's cattle had not gone out this way, he broke camp and rode back to Hinton's cabin, coming in at dusk.

"I'm glad you're back," Hinton said worriedly. "I never saw another place where the wilderness seems to flow out of the country like it does up here."

"It's wild all right, and I never saw a cow." Mack made

a gesture of futility. "I wish George Queen had taken that ride."

That evening they talked of everything except Lou Kyle and Rosella, but mostly about the cattle theft.

"It's got to be the Carnes," Hinton said. "I always arrive at that conclusion by the process of elimination."

"You're shore hipped on the idea," Mack grumbled.

"Next time you ride this way, I'll have evidence." Hinton picked up a large gray stone that had been leaning against the wall, and tossed it to Mack. "What do you thing of that stuff?"

"Pumice." Mack hefted it. "Weighs about as much as a bushel of feathers."

"I found this piece on the other side of Round Butte. It's actually foam on a lava flow, you know. Formed when Round Butte blew up, I suppose. Sort of a volcanic glass."

"What did you bring it home for?"

"It's fine for cleaning out burned pans."

Mack picked up the pumice again. "Funny country here, Jimmy. They say rock floats and wood sinks. There's petrified wood on the other side of Pioneer Creek."

Hinton had opened the door, and stood there, his eyes on the cone-like blot Round Butte made against the sky. Suddenly he turned, shut the door, and came close to where Mack sat.

"Mack," he said, his voice charged with emotion, "I've done a lot of talking about not caring whether I lived, or died next week. I thought I meant it, but now I know I didn't. When I saw you standing there with a rifle in your hands making six good men out of six tough ones in less time than I could whistle, I got a different idea about life."

"Now hold onto your lines!" Mack began.

"This fight you're into with Kyle isn't just for you or Rosella," Hinton went on. "It's for all the people who have been squeezed and perhaps killed because of Kyle's greed. I want to help fight him, and the best weapon I have is money. This cabin is built over a cave, and if I die suddenly, I want you to go into it, and use the funds I have for whatever purpose you see fit.

"If you have to hire an army, hire an army. If this country has to be tamed by violence, use violence. It's everybody's fight. It's going on all over the world. It's humanity against evil. This is just a skirmish, but you've got to win it!"

Mack said nothing more about Hinton coming to town. He shook hands with him the next morning and rode away. Once he looked back and lifted a hand in farewell. He had this last look at his friend, the feeling in him that he would never see this strange, brilliant man alive again.

CHAPTER 8

The End of a Dream

It was the middle of the afternoon when Mack reached Ax-handle. As he made the turn into Main Street surprise jolted an audible exclamation from him. There were more people in town than he had ever seen before. Flags fluttered in the stiff afternoon breeze. Rigs and horses lined both sides of the street. Cattlemen from the West Sundowns, dry farmers from the valley, townspeople—all of them stood in tight little knots along the boardwalk or shouldered their way through the crowd.

Mack reined into the stable.

"What's hit this town?" he asked.

"Some big mogul from the railroad is here to make a speech," the hostler told him.

Mack went along the runway and as he came into the street, a bull voice roared:

"Speech-making about to start! Free coffee, compliments of Lou Kyle! This way, folks!"

Lou Kyle wouldn't give coffee away if it didn't turn him a profit, Mack thought, as he watched the slow drift of the crowd. Then Dad Perrod, standing in the doorway of the feed store, saw him.

"Come here, Mack!" Dad called. When Mack came up, Perrod stepped aside. "Take a look, son, and see what yuh think."

The store was empty. Mack, standing in the doorway, could not believe what he saw. Perrod's lips came away from tooth-less gums in a wide grin as he saw the look of blank amaze-ment come into Mack's face.

"We ain't got a forkful of hay left," Perrod said. "Feller came in a couple of days ago, and bought everything we had. Little better'n five hundred dollars. I put it in the bank."

"Who was he?"

"Don't know."

"My guess is he's buyin' for Kyle," Mack said.

"I kind of figgered that." Perrod shifted uncomfortably. "Fact is, they hauled everything to Kyle's warehouse."

Mack stepped to the door and pulled the sign down. He stared at the board for a time, and read aloud the words, "JARVIS FEED STORE," his mind reaching back over the months and recalling the promise it once had held. In a sud-den gust of temper, he split the board across his knee, threw the fragments the length of the empty room, and wheeled out of the store.

He drifted along the street and made the turn into the lot where the crowd had gathered. He stood there on the outer fringe of it, a lanky, taciturn man with a week's dark stubble on his face, and a layer of dust over him that added a somber tone to the shabby range clothes. His face held a gauntness, a tensity that was not usually a part of him.

Lou Kyle was on the platform, a stocky, handsome man dressed in a black suit and white shirt, black hair perfectly combed, dark eyes flashing as he talked.

"This is the greatest day in Axhandle's history!" Kyle was saying. "On this day we have the promise of the Pioneer Valley Railroad Company that steel will be laid into our city within a year, or eighteen months at the most. You folks who have pioneered this country know the resources that are here.

You folks have blazed the way, have taken the chances that all pioneers must take.''

Kyle spoke on at length. Mack, seeing Inky, moved over to him.

"It's a hot wind from the desert today," he said.

"Yeah, and I'm looking at the gent who's blowing it up," Inky said.

Kyle introduced the railroad man, a bald, heavy-featured man whose bony face was hideously ugly.

"Wonder where they found that?" Inky muttered.

"They scraped the bottom of the barrel for shore," Mack answered.

"To Yance Bishop," Kyle was saying "we owe the completion of the Pioneer Valley Railroad. Ladies and gentlemen, our thanks for Yance Bishop!''

A thunderous clapping rose from those next to the platform. It came, Mack saw, largely from the townsmen, Kyle's close following.

Massive Tash Terris was there. So, too, were the hotel man, the manager of the Mercantile, and a dozen more—all of them business men whose fortunes were closely tied up with Kyle's. Then Mack saw, and was surprised, that Cat Carne was with them.

Little or no clapping came from the bulk of the audience. The dry farmers and the cowmen from the West Sundowns had been bled white by the high prices in the Mercantile and by exorbitant freight rates. It was natural that they should look with suspicion upon anything Kyle said or did.

"Ladies and gentlemen," Yance Bishop boomed, "it gives me great pleasure to bring you the good wishes of the Pioneer Valley Railroad Company, and to tell you that old promises are being kept this day. I want to congratulate you upon having in your midst a great man like Lou Kyle, a man whose heart and soul is in the building of this community.''

"He needs a pitchfork to spread that stuff," Mack muttered.

"He's standing knee deep in it," Inky whispered. "I'm

not going to put this on the pages of the Axhandle Weekly Times. It would corrupt the press so it never would run.''

"Today Axhandle has but a handful of people," Bishop was shouting. "I venture to say that within a year Axhandle will have five thousand. Homesteaders will flock into the high desert. Wheat will grow where bunchgrass stands now as high as a horse's withers. They will plow up the bunchgrass. They will—''

"The devil they will!" George Queen's strident voice cut into Bishop's words. "That high desert is Tomahawk range, and it's goin' to stay Tomahawk range. You bring in a bunch of sodbusters, and we'll hang 'em. By glory, we'll hang you with 'em!''

"Shut up, George!" Wade bellowed.

Bishop pinned his gaze on Queen, a look of injured dignity on his bony face.

"Young man, I've built railroads all my life. I've helped make it possible for the homeseeker to come into our great West and till its fertile soil. I've seen arrogant and powerful cattle companies try to hold the settlers out. For a moment they have succeeded, but only for a moment. The settlers have come, making the desert blossom like a rose. Wheat for miles and miles, wheat—''

"You're crazy!" Queen howled. "How's a man goin' to grow wheat on the desert?''

"If it will grow bunchgrass it will grow wheat. Now if this ignorant cowhand will permit me, I shall go on with my remarks. The railroad will bring wealth to this land such as none of you have foreseen in your wildest dreams. You cattlemen will make a fortune from the sale of beef. The market will be between here and Minter City in the stomach of every railroad laborer.''

"I'm sick," Mack choked. "I'm leaving.''

"I've got to stay and listen," Inky grumbled. "He might say something that has sense in it before he gets done.''

"You're fooling yourself," Mack murmured as he turned away.

Mack returned to the feed store, built a fire, and heated water. Before he had finished shaving, Dad Perrod came in.

"Where we goin' to live?" Perrod asked. "You reckon the bank will be takin' the store building now that we ain't got a store?"

"We'll pitch a tent in the middle of Main Street," said Mack.

"Good idea." Perrod sliced a chew off his plug of tobacco. "We'll put her right in front of Kyle's bank."

"I've been thinking of something else," Mack said slowly. He began stropping his razor, forehead wrinkled in thought. "I'd counted on this feed store making us a stake, which it didn't."

"Five hundred dollars," Perrod pointed out.

"Which ain't much, Dad, but it'll help us get started. I had a hunch while I was listening to the railroad windbag blow off. I was thinking about buying a bunch of steers from the little fellers in the Sundowns and driving 'em to some central place along the right of way. We could butcher 'em, and peddle the beef."

"Good idea," Perrod agreed. "You'd better go see that windbag."

"I aim to, but first I'm going over to Betty's and get me a piece of beef that'll reach from one end of my stomach to the other."

Apparently the speaking was over by the time Mack reached the restaurant, for the crowd was eddying back along Main Street. Mack found an empty stool at the kitchen end of the counter. A moment later the full crest of the crowd hit the restaurant, wedged tight in the door and spilled out along the boardwalk.

"Steak?" Betty asked, and when Mack nodded, she hurried on into the kitchen.

Mack, watching Betty move swiftly and gracefully from customer to kitchen and back, suddenly realized that he had never really seen her before. She had been a shadow in the background of his mind, the picture of Rosella crowding her out.

Now Mack saw her fully, her brown eyes, her hair so dark that it held a sheen in the glow of the lamp she had just lighted. She was short, a head shorter than Rosella, and she was pretty, but it was not a beauty as perfectly cast as Rosella's. There was a scattering of freckles on the tip of her nose, and a long, white scar ran above her left eyebrow.

"I'm a man of leisure," Mack said when she brought his steak.

"So I heard," Betty said. "I wish I had some leisure."

"You're making your fortune."

"What good is a fortune?"

Betty filled her arms with dirty dishes and disappeared into the kitchen.

CHAPTER 9

Love Has No Price

Just as soon as Mack finished eating, he shouldered through the crowd, forcing his way to the street. There he paused, twisted a cigarette, and stood for a time watching the crowd drift aimlessly. Early dusk had come to the town and lights bloomed along the street. Here and there a rig pulled away from the hitch poles. Horses' hoofs struck pistol-sharp on the bridge that crossed Pioneer Creek as families took the valley road out of town.

A poignance struck sharply into Mack Jarvis as life eddied around him. This he wanted: a wife and children, a home, a solid and respected place in the community. Rosella was there in his mind again, centering this desire and refusing to go away. He threw his cigarette into the street, walked rapidly to the hotel, and asked for Yance Bishop.

"Room Twenty-two," the clerk said.

"Thanks."

Mack nodded, and went swiftly up the stairs and past Rooms 16 and 18 which Soogan Wade kept rented for the times when he and Rosella came to town. Mack knocked on the door of Room 22.

"You're a fool, Bishop," he heard Cat Carne say loudly, "for sayin' anything about beef in that speech of yours!"

"Don't call me a fool," Bishop growled, and walked heavily to the door. He opened it a bare six inches, his ugly face showing in the narrow crack. He stared at Mack, hostility stamped upon him. "What do you want?"

"You mentioned the railroad laborers furnishing a market for beef," Mack said. "I'd like to talk to you about it."

"That's been taken care of," Bishop said shortly.

He started to shut the door, but Mack put his shoulder to it and shoved. Bishop, unprepared and entirely surprised by this maneuver, went back, lurched drunkenly for a moment and fell, hitting the floor as hard as a man would twice his weight.

Mack came in, eyes raking the room. Cat Carne stood in the corner, a cigarette dangling from his lips, green eyes amused. Tash Terris sat on the bed beside Lou Kyle. The giant half rose, stared at Bishop, then lifted his eyes to Mack. He straightened, his great hands raising to poise in front of him, his fingers spread.

"Want I should give it to him now, Boss?" Terris asked.

"Sit down," Kyle said testily.

Bishop got up, swearing fiercely as he dusted himself off.

"I have a mind to have you arrested for breaking and entering," he said darkly.

"I want to know why you won't talk business with me," Mack said flatly.

Bishop caught Kyle's eye, and nodded.

"I have just signed a contract with Mr. Kyle for all the meat our camps will need," he said quickly.

"I understand Kyle is going to deliver your horse feed, too."

"That's right."

"Why, you polecat!" Mack exploded. "Do you think Kyle is the only business man in Axhandle?"

"We contract with men who have the financial backing and the moral integrity to deliver whatever their contract calls for," Bishop said.

"That's funny, mister," Mack said hotly. "Moral integrity and Lou Kyle are strangers."

"You'd better go now, Jarvis," Kyle said thickly.

Mack's grin was a quick, wicked slash across his face.

"I heard you offered a thousand dollars to the gent who beefs me. Right, Lou?"

"It's a lie!" Kyle snarled.

Cat Carne was on his feet, his skinny body loose, the smoke from his cigarette a blue shadow before his face.

"I'm sorry I didn't plug you that day on the rim, Jarvis!" he said. "Now I'm giving you two hours to get out of town."

Mack stared at him, thinking there was no sense at all in this kind of challenge, and wondering what lay behind it.

"You scare me, Carne," he said casually. "I'm sure going to run like all get-out."

Mack stepped into the hall, and closed the door.

Rosella Wade was standing in the doorway of her room when Mack came opposite it.

"Come in, Mack," she said softly. "I've been wanting to see you."

Mack stepped into the room. Rosella closed the door, and moved past him to stand beside the bureau. The lamp on the bureau top put a glow upon her hair. Her lips were full and red and expectant as if she knew she had the power to bring him to her. There was here, before Mack's eyes, the reality of a picture that had been in his mind so much. And this moment all the old hunger was in him again.

He moved to her, put his arms about her, and looked into her face. He knew that they were remembering the same things, that she, too, was stirred by those memories. For a short time he held her that way, the old, sweet recklessness upon them. He was thinking about the time they had stood beside the swift turmoil of Pioneer Creek and he had told her he loved her. She had said she could not marry him without her father's permission, but that she would wait for him.

The past lay hard upon him, forming a bond that held them together, and as suddenly was broken into fragments that had no holding power at all. A broken promise was worse than no promise. She brought her hands up to his shoulders, and as she did, the lamplight fell upon her diamond, the sparkle of it bright and sharp and challenging. He stepped away from her and watched disappointment shadow her face, watched the anger grow in it, and bring its scarlet to her face.

"What's the date?" he asked.

"We haven't set it." She paused, setting herself now against him.

"There has not been a day in the past year when you have not been in my mind." He spread his hands as if trying to shove the thought of her away from him. "It's like a tree that's rooted there."

"I'm glad." The anger had gone from her.

"Soogan was right when he said I'd never make a go of the store." Bitterness was in his voice, and he wondered why he went on loving a woman who was promised to another man.

"I'm going back to Tomahawk tomorrow," Rosella said. Her words were a frank invitation.

"Lou Kyle's your man," Mack said sharply. "Don't your promise to him mean any more to you than your promise to me?"

"Because I'm marrying him doesn't mean I'll never speak to another man!" Rosella cried.

"I've got a hunch you'll get a new slant on Kyle after you marry him. Go ahead. Make a mess of your life like you have mine."

"I haven't made a mess of yours!" she flared. "You seem to have developed an appetite for the food in the Top Notch."

"Been listening?"

"It's no secret."

"You care?"

"No. She'll make you a good cook, and she'll be glad to get out of waiting on a hundred men a day."

"I wouldn't say that."

"I didn't mean it that way," Rosella said. "But she isn't pretty."

"I think she is."

Mack started toward the door, and stopped. Someone was rapping a pair of heavy knuckles upon it. Mack whirled to face Rosella.

"Mebbe I'd better crawl under the bed."

"It's just Lou."

Rosella stepped past Mack, and opened the door.

It was Kyle. He looked at Mack, and anger laid a hot shine upon his face.

"I didn't know you had company, Rosella."

"He was just leaving," the girl said lightly.

"Are you ready?"

"I'm ready." She smiled at Mack. "We're having supper with some Axhandle people tonight. Dad will be there, and Yance Bishop, and some more. I wish you were coming."

"I guess not," Mack said, and moved into the hall. "I heard about a bull that got into a kitchen once. He didn't fit."

Kyle moved to the stairs. Rosella turned, and went with him, her hand upon his arm.

"It's foofaraw she likes," Mack thought. "If that's what she wants, he's the right man for her."

The bitterness of the thought was acid in his brain. Kyle had the polish; he had the money. Rosella, looking to the years ahead, had bought what she wanted.

Mack was still standing at the head of the stairs when Kyle came back. He did not speak until he was within three feet of Mack, and when he did, his voice held a fury he had not let Rosella hear.

"I should have killed you a long time ago, Jarvis. When I found you in Rosella's room, I knew I'd waited too long. While you're around here, I'll only have half a woman, and that isn't enough for me."

"So you'll have me beefed if I stay."

"That's right."

Mack laughed, the sound of it a slap across Kyle's wide face.

"You know blame well I won't run. Why don't we smoke

it out, and save somebody else the trouble of wasting good lead on me?"

Kyle shrugged meaty shoulders. "It strikes me that a man's a fool to do his own shooting when he can buy another man's gun to do the job."

"You can't buy everything, Kyle. You can't buy Rosella's love, and you can't pay me enough to get me out of Axhandle. I aim to see that some folks get a square deal out of you who haven't been getting it."

"You think it's smart to hang around and get yourself a slug from an alley just on the off chance you might get somebody a square deal?"

"It's smart enough to make me take the chance of getting that slug," Mack retorted.

"Look, Jarvis." There was desperation in Kyle's voice that was not like him. "You know I can do things for Rosella you never can. If you love her, why don't you pull out?"

"Because I don't think a coyote ever took off his skin and walked like a man," Mack said bluntly.

Kyle's voice was cold and without expression. "You won't be around to see about that. In a little over an hour Cat Carne will kill you."

Kyle left then, moving swiftly down the stairs, and across the lobby. Mack thought about Metolius Neele saying it was worth a thousand dollars to kill him, and about Cat Carne's challenge, and wondered how far ahead it had been planned.

As he left the hotel he saw the buggy that carried Rosella and Kyle make a turn at the end of the street and disappear.

He knew that he should hate her, but he could not.

CHAPTER 10

Monopoly or Freedom

Confusion that was strange to him was in Mack as he drifted along the boardwalk to Inky Blair's printshop. Most of his life he had drifted. He had known his good times; he had taken what was his and had gone on. There was that streak of wildness in him.

He had spoken to Kyle as if he were certain of himself and of what he had to do. He was not. He wasn't sure he even knew what he wanted. Perhaps the drifting life was his, the sky for a blanket, his saddle for a pillow, and purple twilight washing across the sage.

He came into Inky's shop, still thinking about it. He saw Inky look up from his desk, saw his friend's wide-lipped smile.

"You just got here in time to tell me what you think of an editorial I'm going to write," Inky said. "Mister, I'm fixing to blow the lid off."

Then Mack knew. He hated Lou Kyle for the things the man stood for and believed, the things he did to those who came under his power. But there were more important things

to do than hate. One of those was to fight, and there was
plenty of that to do.

"Have at her, boy." Mack reached for a cigar in the box
on Inky's desk. "What set you off?"

"Listening to that hogwash Kyle and Big Ugly got off this
afternoon. Good glory, Kyle will see to it that nobody but he
will make anything out of the railroad. Wouldn't surprise me
if he owned the cussed thing."

Mack pulled up a chair and sat down.

"What do you think Kyle's going to be doing right after
you kick the lid off with an editorial?"

"I don't know." Inky got up and began pacing the floor,
his fat face without color. "I don't mind telling you I'm
scared."

"Then why kick up a bunch of dust?"

"Because Kyle figures me for a walking hunk of fat with
jelly for a backbone. The worst of it is he's right. I've got to
the place where I've either got to fight, or quit looking at
myself in the mirror."

Mack brought a match to life and held the flame to his
cigar. When he had it going, he took it out of his mouth and
blew a series of smoke rings across the desk.

"Inky," he said, "I sure wouldn't keep a man from fighting when he feels like you do, but don't go off half-cocked.
You're our ace of trumps, and I don't want to lose you."

"What do you mean?" Inky asked.

After Mack had told him what had happened at Jimmy
Hinton's homestead, and about Yance Bishop saying that Kyle
had both the horse feed and beef contracts, Inky shook his
head.

"They've started grading between here and Minter City,"
he told Mack, "and Kyle has already sent several loads of
meat to the camps, but I didn't know he had the contracts."

"Now about this editorial," Mack said thoughtfully. "I
said you're our ace because you're the one who mebbe can
work Kyle into the open. If we set pat we're licked. My idea
is for you to worry him. Needle him. Start off with an edi-

torial about what his freight monopoly's doing to the country.''

''I don't see what good it'll do,'' Inky grumbled. ''I want to really blow off.''

''It'll set folks to thinking.'' Mack rose. ''If we had somebody with a little capital, we'd start our own freight line between here and the Columbia, and that'd be something Kyle would sure enough worry about.''

''Who's got any capital?'' Inky snorted.

''I've got a notion.''

Mack moved to the door, and stood there, his eyes on his friend, his thought a swift, chill stream. It was only a matter of minutes until he'd be facing Cat Carne's gun. ''Once you head for some place, pardner,'' he murmured, ''keep your eyes ahead. Don't ever look back.''

''It was Lot's wife who looked back, wasn't it?''

''Never knew the lady.''

Inky grinned. ''It's from the Bible.''

''What happened to her?''

''She turned to salt.''

''You'd turn to lard,'' Mack said, and went into the street.

Mack moved along the street to the end of it and turning, looked back upon it. This town had been his home. It was the first time in his life he had ever called a town home. But he did not belong here, and he felt it now more keenly than ever before.

He stood pulling at his cigar, tasting it and enjoying the fragrance of it, and feeling suddenly the joy there was in living. There were many good things in life. The memory of them swept through him now, and he wondered, as man has since the beginning of time, why there is so much misery and strife in a world that holds so much beauty.

Axhandle lay before him, blanketed by night, Main Street a dusty path between two rows of stiff, false-fronted buildings. Along it lights burst from windows of the Casino, the hotel, Inky Blair's printshop, Betty's restaurant.

Here were common people, decent people who asked nothing of life but to be allowed to live and earn that which was by right theirs. Over it lay the shadow of one grasping, selfish man who schemed carefully and slowly and wickedly, and because there was little courage in this town, that scheming had gone unchallenged until now.

Kyle had not questioned Carne's ability to outdraw Mack and kill him. Mack realized, then, that he had been letting his thoughts run along that same fatal pattern. In his own mind he was dead.

"Don't ever look back." He had told Inky that, yet now he found himself doing exactly the thing he had told Inky not to do. He was looking back along his life, thinking of Rosella Wade who would soon be Rosella Kyle, and closing the book of his future, exactly as his romance with Rosella had been closed.

With a muttered oath, Mack tore the cigar from his mouth, and threw it into the dust. He pulled his gun from holster, gave the cylinder a quick whirl and, with the Colt riding easily in leather, turned and went again along the street.

There were a dozen men in the Casino, most of them cowmen from the West Sundowns who knew Mack from trading with him through the past year. They nodded when he came in, noted the gray grimness of his face, and held their silence. Mack strode past them and went on to the far end of the bar. There he turned, faced the batwings, and waited.

The seconds ticked off in a slow, nerve-stretching rhythm. More than two hours had passed. This wait was like Cat Carne. He would set a time, and then be late, thinking the suspense would crack his enemy's nerve.

It was half an hour after Mack had come into the Casino before the batwings opened and slapped shut behind Cat Carne. He came in to stand under an overhead lamp, its down-thrown cone of light bringing out with striking sharpness the catlike cruelty that was on his thin face. He stood there slouched a little, all loose of joint, green eyes making a swift study of the room and then fixing on Mack.

"I gave you two hours to get out of town," he snarled. "It's that and past, Jarvis. Why ain't you gone?"

Mack's grin streaked across his dark face.

"I never obey the order of a smoke-eatin' gunslick, Carne. Besides, I aim to dig out the scheming son who paid you to kill me."

Then Mack stepped away from the bar and paced slowly toward Cat Carne.

A man at the bar cried out involuntarily, and ducked behind it. Others braced themselves and stood without motion. There was no talk and no noise but the indrawing and expelling of men's breaths. Behind the mahogany the barman coughed, the sound of it brittle-sharp against the quiet.

Cat had counted on the waiting to snap Mack's nerves. Now, seeing that his enemy was not afraid, that his self-control had not broken, Carne became possessed of the sudden and chilling thought that he might be the man to die. There was nothing on his skinny face to show it, nothing in his green eyes or his cold exterior to tell Mack what Carne was thinking, yet he felt what was in the man, and he pressed his advantage.

"I had some respect for you the other day at the gate," Mack said in so low a voice that Carne had to strain to hear. "Mebbe you figured you had something to fight for. But when you do another man's fighting you're getting low enough to walk under your gate when it's closed without touching your hat on the bottom log."

It was then that Mack deliberately took his eyes from Carne and threw a quick glance into the front corner of the saloon as if to signal a man standing there. Cat Carne, always a suspicious, questioning man, turned his head to look. In that same instant he drew his gun. He got in the first shot before Mack's gun was lifted from its casing and leveled, a clear shot that should have smashed life from Mack but did not because Carne's eyes were not on his target.

Then Mack's Colt spilled out a foot-long tongue of flame. The bullet turned Carne partly around so that his second shot was as wild as his first. Mack fired again, the bullet driving into Carne's middle. Carne went back a single step, trying to keep his feet, trying to bring his gun up for a final shot, and failing. He reached behind him to a poker table for support, his hand wobbling uncertainly, and did not find it. Then he fell.

A gusty sigh rose from the men along the bar as if they had seen a thing they had hoped to see and had not thought they would. The man behind the mahogany poked his head into view for a tentative look, and slowly straightened.

Mack walked to where Carne lay, his gun covering the fallen man. When he saw Carne's face he wheeled away and went back to the bar where he had been standing when Carne came in. He poured a drink and took it, and stood there while weakness took possession of him.

These last hours had built to a peak. Now he was over it and going down the opposite side. Always it was this way after a shooting affair. The fury had gone out of him, the fire and the tenseness. He wondered when there would be peace in his life, when he would not see death or have the smell of powdersmoke in his nostrils.

The medico came and took Carne's body away. Inky Blair and Soogan Wade stood a yard from Mack, and when he felt their presence, he motioned toward the bottle.

Natty Gordon had been talking to the men who had seen the fight. Now he moved toward Mack.

"They tell me you was waitin' for Carne, and that he came in and jumped yuh," he said. "That right?"

"Right." Mack poured another drink. "Disappointed?"

"No," Gordon answered, in the manner of one covering his real feelings, "but I'd like to know what this was all about. I'm glad enough to see Carne dead. He was a bad one. Pulled off three killings since I've been deputy here, and every time he made the other hombre draw first. The boys say he got in the first and missed. Then you plugged him."

"His luck was bad. As to what it was all about, I don't know. He told me I had two hours to get out of town. I ain't one to run, Natty."

"I reckon you ain't," Gordon admitted grudgingly. "Why did he tell you to get out of town?"

Mack shrugged. "I've got a notion which you wouldn't believe and I can't prove, so I'll keep it to myself."

"All right."

"Wait a minute," Mack said, as the deputy started to turn away. "I want your help in the morning, Natty."

Gordon swung back. "What kind of help?"

"I want to get into Carne Cove. It'll be legal if you're along."

"That's a fool idea!" Gordon shrilled. "The Carnes don't want nobody monkeyin' around. After what you've just done to Cat, the other boys will plug you on sight!"

"Mebbe," Mack admitted. "The point is they don't act like law-abiding people. If they were, why should they be so ornery about keepin' folks out?"

Gordon scratched his head. "I always wondered about it, but from what I hear, the old man was just cantankerous. Wanted to live by himself, so he homesteaded down there in a hole in the ground. I guess the boys took after him."

"There's something else to it than being ornery. If there wasn't, why would they put up that log gate on the rim, and why would one of them stand guard all the time?"

"I've always had a notion," Wade cut in, "that they was runnin' an outlaw hideout."

"That's my hunch," Mack agreed. "Natty, you going with me?"

Gordon shook his head. "Not till I've got something definite to go on."

"Natty, you're the poorest excuse for a law officer I ever saw," Mack said angrily. "You're going with me, or I'll get a handful of sand and pound it into your skull with the barrel of my forty-five!"

Gordon swallowed, looked appealingly at Wade, and nodded.

"All right. In the morning."

He made a quick turnabout, and half-ran from the saloon.

CHAPTER 11

A Bargain With Soogan Wade

Gordon's attitude brought first puzzlement, then anger to the face of old Soogan Wade. He watched the lawman go, cursing steadily and fiercely.

"No wonder nothin's done about my cows," he muttered then. "One of these days I'm goin' to take me a ride to the county seat and blacksnake the hombre who calls himself a sheriff. Why he keeps a dude like Gordon down here as deputy is something I'd like to know."

"I've been wondering if mebbe Kyle was the reason," Mack said.

Wade looked at him sharply. "Why should he be?"

"Just an idea. Politics somewheres. Mebbe we ought to send for the sheriff."

"He wouldn't come," Wade grumbled. "He's fatter'n you are, Blair."

Inky pinned his eyes on Mack. "That was good shooting, son, but you didn't have any real reason to risk your hide fighting that gunslick."

"Sometimes you've got to skim the foam off before you can get at the stuff you want," reminded Mack.

"Maybe. Now you'd be smart to go home and to bed. Skimming the foam off is enough of a chore for one night."

"I reckon." Mack gave his friend a quick grin. "I kind of wanted this mess to jell so's we can see what we've got."

"What kind of fool beating-about-the-bush gab is this?" Wade shouted.

"Plain English, Soogan." Inky grinned at Wade. He started to move away, then turned back. "I forgot to tell you, Mack, that when you were gone, the Carnes started hauling hay into town to Kyle's warehouse. Awful small loads for some reason."

"Mighty hard pull up that grade," Wade suggested.

"Graders have started moving dirt between here and Minter City," Inky went on, "and Kyle's sending beef to the camps. I saw a couple of loads go out yesterday about dusk. Couple more went out tonight."

Mack nodded, watching Wade to see if Inky's talk made any sense to him, but he saw only a puzzled frown. Inky left.

"Rosella told me you're eating with the top crust tonight," Mack said to Soogan Wade.

"Naw. I don't know how to act in front of them folks."

Mack drank his whisky and pushed the bottle toward Wade. The old man had aged a year in the last week, Mack thought. Wade stood toying with one of the gold coins on his coat, his usual arrogant belligerence gone.

"You've got nerve," he said to Mack. "I wish you was riding for the Tomahawk again."

"I had the notion you didn't hold much affection for me."

"I didn't like the way you hung around Rosella. Now that she's taken, I reckon you'll let her alone."

"You offering me a job?"

"You ain't got a store," Wade said defensively. "I thought you'd be lookin' for a job."

"I need a job all right, but I figure I'm worth more'n thirty a month and beans, which same is a point I guess we don't agree on."

"Shucks, I ain't goin' to fire George just to give you a good job."

"I don't want George's job, Soogan. I want to find your cows, and I want five hundred dollars for doing it."

"That's a deal," Soogan said eagerly.

"There's one joker in the deal, Soogan. You're going to tell your boys to leave Jimmy Hinton alone. He ain't doing you no hurt."

"Like sin he ain't!" Wade bellowed. "He turned a spring into a hog waller."

"That ain't enough to run a man out of his home for."

Wade held his silence for a time, a blunt finger tracing a Tomahawk pattern on the bartop.

"All right," he finally said. "I'll give you till fall."

"And you're going with me and Natty in the morning just on the off chance we might see something in the Cove."

"Shore. I'll go for the ride." Wade's eyes narrowed. "You tryin' to say my cows are in the Cove?"

"Long as we're down there, we might as well look around."

"I've been plumb to the bottom," Wade said flatly, "and you couldn't hide a week-old calf in that danged hole that you couldn't see from the rim. Get the notion out of your head."

Wade nodded, and left the saloon.

It was then that the cowmen moved toward Mack, and made a half-circle around him.

"It ain't no secret you're buckin' Kyle, Jarvis," one of them said. "We're in the same boat. Seems smart for us to get together."

"It would be." Mack reached into his pocket for paper and tobacco.

"Until the railroad gets here," the man went on, "we'll keep on paying the freight Kyle charges us, and with him puttin' the squeeze on us through the bank, the railroad ain't going to get here in time."

"Go on." Mack shaped up his smoke, and returned the tobacco and paper to his pocket.

"Well, cuss it," the man said, "we stand to lose everything we've got!"

"You'd lick Kyle if you had your own freighting outfit," Mack said.

"No good." The cowman shook his head. "Nobody around here would put up money we'd need to buy wagons and teams."

"There is a way," a man next to the bar said. "I seen it done in Idaho once. Form a buyers' association. We'd delegate somebody like Jarvis to do our buying and the association would pay him a salary."

"You can't roll stuff uphill from Columbia," the first man said doggedly. "We'd still need wagons and teams."

"We've all got wagons, we've got teams, and by Jehoshaphat, I say it would be worth it to take time enough to go to Columbia. You've been running a store, Jarvis. What do you say?"

"Sure. I'll take the job." Mack didn't let his face indicate the swift flow of elation that washed through him. "I'll have Inky Blair run off some order blanks tomorrow. In a few days I'll take a swing up through the Sundowns and you can sign up."

They nodded, these sun-darkened, bitter men who saw disaster running uncomfortably close. For a moment there was hope in them, and then it faded as they thought about Kyle, and the things he had done.

"When Kyle hears this," one said, "he'll come up with some dirty scheme that'll fix us."

"Mebbe not," Mack said, and left the saloon.

There was no light in the block now except that from the Casino. A cold wind hurrying along the street from the Sundowns sent a shiver down Mack's spine. Turning toward the feed store that was no longer a feed store, he wondered what Kyle would say when he heard about the buyers' association.

Abruptly shadowy figures came at him from the darkness of an alleyhead, how many of them he didn't know. They swarmed over him. He tried to get his gun, and could not reach it. He struck out with his fists, felt flesh under his knuckles, and heard a man curse. Then something hit him on the head, taking the light from his eyes and the strength from his knees. He would have gone down if a great arm had not caught him.

"That's all, boys!" a voice said.

Mack did not know how much time passed. He never went completely out. There was a whirling blackness streaked with red. He knew he was being carried, that later he was thrown on a floor, and that a wall lamp was brought to life. The blackness fell away like fog breaking suddenly from the earth and leaving the sun full upon it. He sat up, rubbed an aching head, and placed his back to the wall.

It was a single-room cabin, Mack saw. There was a bed at one end, the dirty blankets twisted into a gray, patternless mass.

At the other end was a stove, table and two chairs. Shades were pulled over the two windows.

He had this little glance before he saw the great figure of a man sitting in the shadows next to the stove. A laugh rumbled from the man's throat. Mack tried to bring himself to his feet, but he had not the strength for it. He fell back against the wall, hopelessness pressing through his aching head. The man was Tash Terris.

Terris rose from his seat beside the stove, shook his great body, and lumbered to the center of the cabin. He stood motionless for a moment, beady eyes filled with triumph, meaty lips pulled away from yellow teeth in a wicked grin. Mack, his back pressed against the wall, stared up into the brutal face, and could see no hope for anything but a cruel death.

"You know what I'm goin' to do?" Terris asked craftily. "I'll tell you. I'm goin' to kill you dead." He went back to the stove and picked up a length of pine limb. "I'm goin' to take you down to the creek and crack your skull with this. Then I'll throw you in, and everybody'll think you just got hurt and fell in."

It sounded more like Lou Kyle's scheming than any idea that would rise in Tash Terris' minuscule brain, and it might work just about the way Kyle planned. Mack's eyes made a quick search of the cabin, but there was no gun in sight. The nearest thing to a weapon was an ax leaning against the wall at the other end of the wood box, but it was across the room from Mack, and he had no hope of reaching it with Terris standing in front of him.

"You aiming to kill me here, or down by the creek?" he asked.

"Down by the creek."

Mack laughed. "You'll never get me down there, Tash. I'll yell my head off as soon as I get out of here, and I'll have the whole town awake. If you was as smart as you think you are, you'd tear a piece of one of them blankets"—he motioned toward the bed—"and put a gag in my mouth before we start."

"Yeah, that's a good idea. I'll do it."

Terris plodded to the bed and tore a long strip from a dirty blanket. Then he straightened up, a new and puzzling thought coming into his brain and setting up its disturbance there.

"Why are you tellin' me what to do?" he growled. "If you open your mouth to holler, I'll fix you!"

He turned to look at Mack, but Mack was not on the floor where the big man had left him. He had reached the stove and had the ax in his hands before Terris saw him. The giant bellowed like a thwarted bull and came at Mack.

"Stand still," Mack shouted, "or I'll bust your head open!"

But nothing could have stopped Tash Terris then. He rushed Mack, huge hands outstretched. For an instant Mack did not move. Terris raised one hairy arm in front of his face to ward off the ax. He kept the other arm in front of his chest, hand balled into a clublike fist.

It was impossible to drive an effective blow past that huge arm, and Mack knew that if he failed on the first try he would never get another chance. For Tash Terris was a monstrous, roaring fury who would be satisfied by nothing short of Mack Jarvis' death! So Mack, instead of swinging blindly for Terris' head, stepped swiftly aside and brought the ax in a low, upswinging blow against the side of the giant's leg.

Terris hit the stove, crashed with it into the wall, and rolled off to the floor. The stove pipes broke loose and fell across the man, soot streaming out of them and laying a black sprinkle over him. He rolled free, a steady roar of curses pouring from his mouth. He came up on his good leg, threw his weight on the one Mack had struck and fell forward, the cabin rocking with the weight of him.

Mack had reached the door, had unlocked it and jerked it open. He whirled to face Terris and it was then he saw the spurting blood, saw the agony on the giant's face and knew he could safely and without trouble kill Terris.

"If you was in my boots, Tash," he said, "you'd use this ax to split my head open."

Terris lay on his stomach, his head raised, a whimper of fear coming from him.

"Mack!" It was a girl's voice, sweet and clear, and utterly unexpected. "Mack, you all right?"

Betty Grant stepped into the light flowing through the open doorway. She carried a gun in her hand, and when she heard Mack say, "I'm fine," she called, "Here he is, Dad!"

"How did you happen to be out looking for me?" Mack demanded.

"I'll tell you later."

Betty looked at Terris and quickly turned away.

Dad Perrod came into the light, and a moment later Inky Blair was there.

"We ought to let this ornery son bleed to death, but I guess we can't," Mack said. He took Perrod's shotgun from him, fired a blast into the night silence, and gave the gun back. "That'll bring 'em. Dad, you'd better stay around."

Perrod nodded, and slipped into the shadows.

CHAPTER 12

Inside the Cove

Hurrying along an alley back to town, Mack told Betty Grant and Inky what had happened. Before they reached the restaurant, they saw bobbing lanterns in the street, and heard shouted questions.

"Tash Terris has got a leg plumb near cut off!" somebody yelled.

"You going to have Terris arrested?" Inky asked.

"No," Mack answered. "With that leg the way it is, he won't be bothering us for awhile, and I'm kind of curious to see what he says about how he got it. Likewise what Kyle will do now that two of his bully boys have petered out."

"He'll do plenty," Betty said bitterly, as she unlocked her back door. "Come in."

"I'd better go over to my place," Mack said.

"You're staying here with me tonight," Betty said firmly. "Don't argue."

"I'm not goin to—"

"Oh yes you are." Inky grinned. "I came up a while ago, and helped her fix a couple of beds in her attic."

"I don't care if you've got a dozen beds, I'm not—"

Betty had lighted a lamp and had gone into her living room.

"Come on in, Mack," she called nervously. "You, too, Inky. I'll make some coffee."

Mack went in reluctantly, and watched Betty put the lamp down and go into the kitchen. Inky paused to say something to her, then followed Mack into the living room.

"The girl's got a touch, hasn't she?" Inky said, looking around.

"Yeah," Mack answered.

He had never been in this room before. There were bright curtains at the windows, a sofa against the wall, and a bowl of violets on the small oak stand. A cutting table and sewing machine stood together at the far end of the room, and on the table was a pile of filmy white material. That, Mack guessed, would be Rosella's wedding dress.

He brought his eyes back to Inky, and nodded.

"Yeah, she's got a touch."

Mack sat down on the sofa, weariness coming upon him suddenly. He leaned his head against the wall and immediately went to sleep. When he woke, Dad Perrod had come in.

"A fellow'd think you'd do your sleeping in bed," Inky said, in pretended indignation.

"Hush," Betty said sharply. She poured a cup of coffee and brought it to him. "Inky says you're going to the Cove in the morning, so we won't keep you long."

"What happened, Dad?" Mack asked.

"Nothin' much. Surprising little, in fact. Doc says Terris won't walk for a spell. Funniest thing was how soon Kyle got there. I never saw a man look madder. Terris started to say somethin' about a scrap, and Kyle says, 'You done it yourself. Don't try to say nothin' else.' "

"Gordon there?" Mack asked.

"Yep. He shore was. Cussin' a blue streak because he was waked up in the middle of the night by a shotgun goin' off. Said it was blame funny Tash had an ax cut on his leg instead of a load of buckshot in his head."

Mack looked at Betty, thought about her searching for him

in the night, a gun in her hand, and when he spoke his voice was more gentle than was his habit.

"Why did you want Dad and me to sleep here?" he asked her.

"I'm scared, Mack," she told him. "And there's another reason that's more important. You'd be safer here." When she saw the scowl darken his face, she added hastily, "I heard something tonight that gave me the biggest scare I ever had. I thought you were asleep in the feed store, but by the time I had Dad awake, I guess Terris had you in his cabin."

"What Kyle's done tonight," Inky cut in, "goes to prove you can't beat him. You've killed Cat Carne and you've bunged Terris up, but what good is it?"

"I'm still alive."

"For the moment. Kyle's showed his hand now. One of these days your luck is bound to run out."

"A man makes his own luck," Mack observed drily. "Betty, what was it you heard?"

"Cat Carne, Terris, and that railroad man Bishop came into the restaurant for some coffee. They talked low so I couldn't hear all they said, but I heard enough to know they were sure you'd be dead before morning. Bishop said if they failed twice, they wouldn't the third time."

"One was Carne," Mack murmured, "and the second was Terris. What's their third ace?"

"Something about burning your store building. Bishop said a crack on the skull would keep you from walking out, and everybody would think you'd burned to death. They'd been in the restaurant about half an hour before Carne left. Bishop and Terris went out when they heard the shooting."

Mack grinned wryly. "You know, Betty, it would be a pretty good world if it wasn't for the people."

Betty glanced at the filmy material for the wedding dress and quickly brought her eyes away.

"It is a good world in spite of the people," she said.

"One gent like Kyle sure smells up the place," Inky growled.

"Dad, I'm sending you to The Dalles in a few days,"

Mack said. "Inky, tomorrow you run off some order blanks. Long ones." He measured with his hands. "My job is to keep alive. I'm thinking it won't be long till Kyle schemes himself into a jackpot he can't get out of. Dad, let's go home."

"Mack, you can't!' Betty cried.

"You stubborn, mule-headed ape!" Inky raged. "Just because you're a fool for luck is no reason everybody else is. If Betty's hurt—"

They were on their feet, facing each other, Mack and Betty. A look he couldn't read was in her dark eyes. She made a gesture as if to hold him, and instantly brought her hands back. He saw then he had pushed her into a begging position, and her pride was too great to let her beg even from him.

"We'll stay," he said humbly.

It was not yet full day when Soogan Wade and Natty Gordon ate breakfast with Mack in the restaurant and when they rode out of town the night chill was all around. They reached the rim and, looking down upon the town, saw the fingers of smoke from newly-made fires standing like sedate blue columns. Behind the Casino a man was chopping wood, the hollow echo of ax biting into pine rising to them.

"For once that burg looks peaceful," Natty Gordon growled. He laid a hostile glance on Mack's face. "That's because you ain't down there."

"You've got no call to blame me," Mack said with sharp anger. "If you were a little piece of a lawman, we wouldn't be in the shape we are."

"And I'd have three hundred cows I don't have," Wade added.

The high, thin air still held its sharp bite when they reached the Carne gate. Gordon swung down and moved the end post to which the gate was locked. A shiver seized him, and whether it came from the cold or from fear Mack could not tell.

Gordon peered through the logs trying to see the bottom of the Cove.

"Mighty long ways down there," he muttered.

As he reached for the padlock, a Winchester tore apart the morning quiet with a sharp, echoing explosion, the bullet slapping into the post less than a foot from Gordon's hands.

There was a courage of sorts in Natty Gordon.

"This is the Law you're shootin' at Carne!" he called. "We want to go down into the Cove for a look. If you refuse to let us in, I'll have to think you're guilty as hell of something!"

The man in the lava made no answer. There was a long silence, with Natty Gordon, gray-faced, watching the rifleman's hiding place with uncertainty, and Mack and Wade sitting their saddles, eyes on the deputy. Presently there was the metallic rattle of wheels on rocks.

"Open up, Dan!" a man below the gate called.

"Hold it!" Dan Carne called, and carefully rose from the lava.

He came warily to the gate, Winchester carried at his hip, the muzzle of it swinging to cover Mack Jarvis as if he thought neither Wade nor Gordon was nothing worth watching.

Dan Carne was heavier and shorter than Cat had been, and his arms were thick and dark with a hair covering. His bulldog jaw gave an appearance of wideness to his face, and in that way he was utterly different in appearance from his younger brother. But his eyes were green, and held the same cruel cunning that had marked Cat's eyes.

He unlocked the padlock, and swung the gate back. A buggy wheeled through. Mack, staring at it in astonishment, saw that it was Lou Kyle's. The team was Kyle's matched bays; the driver was one of Kyle's freighters. He gave Mack a hard, emotionless stare, and drove on.

"All right," Carne said. "You boys can ride through, but the chances are you'll never come back."

Gordon ran a tongue over dry lips, his eyes flickering to Mack as if to see whether Mack had changed his mind about going down. He brought his gaze to Carne.

"If we're goin' to stay down there permanent, Dan," he said, "I hope you've got plenty of beef."

Carne jumped as if he had been stung, his rifle barrel swinging toward Gordon, suspicion whetting his instinctive hatred close to the killing point.

"What yuh mean about plenty of beef?" he demanded.

"I didn't mean nothin'," Gordon said quickly. "I just like beef. Never go for mutton, and pork don't set well on my stomach."

"Then talk to Wade. He's got lots of beef."

Carne shifted his Winchester to Mack. He stood motionless for a time, green eyes filled with a shrewd and murderous cunning. He seemed to be in doubt whether to kill Mack now or later. Apparently he decided to wait, for as he stepped aside, he jerked a thumb down the steep narrow road.

"Start out," he ordered. "If you make a wrong move, I'll put a winder in your back."

They strung out along the road, Gordon in front, then Wade, and finally Mack. Swiftly they reached the Cove floor, for the road they followed was a short one which made a sharp pitch along the east wall of the cliff. Carne followed on foot, and when they reached the bottom, he was but a few feet behind Mack's sorrel.

"Ride over to the house!" he called.

CHAPTER 13

Blank Wall

Obviously it was a womanless place they were approaching. There were no flowers, and no vegetable garden. Chickens and ducks were all over the yard, and from the barn a guinea hen set up her clattering. A black and white hound got to his feet, yawned, and sat down again, giving Mack a hungry look. Three mowers had been drawn up beside the barn, and Mack guessed that the alfalfa was ready for the first cutting.

They reined up close to the front door of the log house, Dan Carne still following.

"You gents think it's three to one," he said, a murderous intent clearly marking his voice, "and that if you're lucky, one of you can get me before I get all three of yuh. You're plumb wrong. There's six men in that house, and before one of yuh could get a hand within two feet of your gun butt, you'd be dead."

And as if to punctuate Dan Carne's words, the ominous sound of guns coming to cock came to them through the still morning air.

Natty Gordon shifted in his saddle.

"We just want to look around, Dan," he pleaded.

"Why?" Carne demanded.

"Well, Mack thought—I mean, cuss it, Dan, it's a funny-lookin' layout. Ain't natural the way you keep folks out."

"I don't see nothin' funny about it," Carne snarled. "If we ant to live by ourselves, it sure ain't nobody's business. Least of all"—he motioned with his rifle barrel—"that killin' son. Us Carnes stomp our own snakes, and we shore aim to stomp that one."

"It was a fair fight he had with Cat," Gordon said quickly.

Dan Carne spat contemptuously. "I don't believe it. All you town buzzards hold together."

"Put that Winchester down," Mack said, "and we'll see if you've got any better luck than Cat had."

"Nope." Carne shook his head. "I'll just drill you where yuh set. Might as well drill Wade and Gordon, too."

"You'd make a bad mistake!" Gordon cried. "A lot of folks know where we came."

"I'll shoot them other folks when they show up," Carne said indifferently, and raised his rifle. "I'll take Jarvis first."

It didn't make sense to Mack, but a lot of things had happened in the last weeks that made less sense. All of it fitted into a logical pattern, and there would come a time, if he lived, when he would see what it was. Right now he was like a man who had gone to sleep, and had started his nightmare in the middle.

"Dan, you got any idea why we're here?" he called sharply.

Carne lowered his rifle. "You're after Tash Terris, ain't yuh?"

"Terris?" Gordon shouted in vast surprise. "Why should we want him?"

"No, we ain't after Terris," Mack said quickly.

Carne cuffed back his battered Stetson, and scratched his head.

"Then why in tunket *are* yuh here?"

"Out of suspicion mostly," Mack answered.

"I've had some letters from the sheriff about some tough hands who drift north from Nevada and hole up somewheres," Gordon said. "We figgered you boys might be furnishin' 'em a hideout."

"Well, we ain't," Carne snarled.

"Who's the six men in the house?" Mack asked.

"Hay hands," Carne leveled the rifle again. "I'm done talkin'."

Mack had expected this, and his hand was slicing downward for his gun when Lou Kyle called from inside the house:

"Hold it, Mack. Dan, put that Winchester up."

Mack let his gun drop back into holster. Carne put his rifle down, and cursed angrily.

"Cuss it, Kyle, just because we've agreed to deliver hay and—er—such don't give yuh no call to boss us!

"Yes, I know what the agreement is," Kyle said grimly.

The banker-promoter came out of the house. He was immaculately clad in a black suit, string tie, and white shirt. His hat was an expensive black Stetson, and when he thrust his hands into his pants' pockets the skirt of his coat came back to show the silverplated, pearl-handled gun that was cased in an elaborate holster.

He stood there wearing a cloak of amiability as easily as he wore his clothes, white teeth showing in a friendly smile. Mack, watching him, wondered what there was about a hay deal that would bring him into the Cove.

A sigh of relief came from Soogan Wade. "I'm glad to see you, Lou." He jabbed a finger at Mack. "That idiot brought us down here on a wild goose chase. Said we'd look around for my cattle, and we damn near got our brains shot out because of it."

Fear put a shadow on Dan Carne's face, and he reached for the .30-30 he had leaned against the porch. Again Mack's fingers were around his gun butt. He saw Kyle make a quick, warning gesture, saw Carne straighten up and put his hands in his pockets.

Pete Carne, another brother, came out of the house and stood beside Kyle. He was a taller man than Dan, and slimmer. His nose was both long and red; his eyes bloodshot and furtive. He was a hard drinker, and his speech was heavy with whiskey when he spoke.

"I don't take to nobody callin' me a cow thief," he said, "and I ain't goin' to stand for it from the coyote who plugged Cat."

"There'll come a day when we settle all debts," Kyle said with mild persuasion. "Since these gents think there are cows in the Cove that don't belong here, I suggest we let them take a look."

"Are yuh loco?" Dan Carne demanded.

There were bits of by-play here that Mack caught—inflections of voice, gestures, the exchange of signals between Kyle and Dan Carne; all building conviction in Mack's mind that the stolen beef was in the Cove, and that Kyle was as deeply involved as the Carnes. These things Mack had noticed would escape both Gordon and Wade, for Wade was letting a slow anger come to a heat in him, and Gordon was too busy thinking how to get out of the Cove with his life to see anything else.

"No, not loco, Dan," Kyle was saying blandly. "For my sake, I want this accusation crammed back into the gullet of the man who made it. Did Jarvis accuse me of having a hand in the stealing of your cows, Soogan?"

"I don't recollect he did," Wade admitted.

"He's been trying to injure me since I announced Rosella's and my engagement," Kyle went on smoothly, "so I thought he might try to blacken my name along with that of the Carne brothers."

"You're a smart one, Lou," Mack said, with a short, dry laugh. "I've got a hunch you're so smart you'll work yourself into a corner."

"We'll see who gets into the corner, my friend." Kyle nodded at Dan Carne. "Let's take these men past the barn, and let them have their look."

"I ain't standing for no snooping," Dan Carne said stubbornly. "You're getting hay here, and you're getting cheap—"

"I'm as interested in keeping them from tramping down

your crops as anybody," Kyle broke in. "We'll let them understand that the next time they show up they'll get shot without talk."

He motioned to Mack and strode around the barn.

Mack turned his sorrel, and rode after Kyle. Gordon followed, and after a moment's hesitation, Wade came. Kyle had paused between a rye field and the barn, but before he could speak, Mack asked:

"Why is Tash Terris here, Lou? You figger he might talk after he didn't make a go of it last night?"

"Your luck's just about run out, Jarvis," Kyle snarled. Then he saw Wade coming, and again assumed the mask of bland courtesy. He pointed upstream. "The Cove floor is of lower altitude than the high desert, it's sheltered by the canyon walls, and the soil is rich. The Carnes take water from the creek and divert it over the land. Those are the reasons why they raise the tremendous alfalfa and grain crops they do. I might also point out that with such a place as the Carne boys have, it certainly would not be necessary for them to resort to stealing cattle or furnishing a hideout for outlaws."

"Always the showoff, ain't you, Lou?" Mack asked contemptuously. "There's something wrong here, and you know what it is. But Natty and Soogan wouldn't believe it if they saw it, so you don't need to shovel it on a yard deep."

"You see, Soogan?" Kyle spread his hands hopelessly. "I've saved his life, and now he accuses me of underhand dealing."

"I'm not accusing you of anything," Mack cut in. "Not yet. All I want to do is look."

"You've looked. Now ride out, and heaven help you if you ever show your face within sight of Carne Cove again." Kyle pointed to the road slanting up the east wall, like a thin knife blade laid along it. "You'd better go now. Dan's feeling plumb proddy."

Wade and Gordon wheeled their horses and rode back to the house.

"Just a minute," Mack said.

He pointed to a long, spinelike ridge a mile up the creek

that ran from the east rim to the Cove floor. A man or a horse could follow that ridge from the rim to the bottom of the Cove with far less difficulty than he could follow the road.

"Is there any farm land beyond that hogback?" he asked.

"No," Kyle said quickly. "That's the north end of the Cove."

Still Mack did not turn his sorrel to follow Gordon and Wade. He was thinking about what he had said to Betty—that it would be a good world if it wasn't for the people. Here was proof of it.

The sun had tipped over the rim and was warming the last of the night chill. It lay brightly upon the alfalfa and grain in eye-glittering brilliance, and sowed diamonds on the white surface of the creek. It brought alive the green and browns and yellows of the canyon walls. Here was beauty in a concentration such as Mack had never seen before, a masterpiece of nature that made him feel as small as an undersized ant in the bottom of a giant coffee cup.

South of Mack and not far from where he sat his saddle the walls of the canyon so nearly touched that there was barely passage room for the creek. It ran in a swift and shouting turbulence that never saw the sun. North of the slanting hogback it would be the same, for he had seen it from the rim when he had been in the East Sundowns. This tight little canyon, set off by itself from the world around it, was a perfect location for the execution of whatever lawless plans Kyle and the Carnes had.

"I'm givin' yuh sixty seconds to get out of the Cove!" Dan Carne called.

"I can't hold him off any longer," Kyle warned.

As Mack turned his sorrel toward the east wall of the Cove, he saw a long haystack set close to the base of the cliff. It was a carryover from the previous summer, browned by wind and rain, and Mack guessed that the hay being hauled to Kyle's warehouse in Axhandle was likely coming from this stack.

It was nearly a mile from the buildings, and it struck Mack that there must have been some reason for placing it in that particular spot. Then he thought no more about it, for he had come up to Soogan Wade, and he saw the cold fury that was in the old cowman.

"You satisfied?" Wade demanded.

"No."

"Well, by Jupe," Wade raged, "what does it take to convince you? You can look down from the rim, and you can't see no cows. Now you're here and you still can't see no cows. You reckon Dan Carne's got 'em in the house?"

"I'm not saying what I think," Mack replied in a cold tone. "If there are cows to be found, I aim to find them."

"Where?" Wade demanded

"Calm down," Mack advised him. "You won't get anywhere by yelling at the top of your lungs. I can hear you quite well."

Wade ground his teeth in anger, but he took Mack's advice and waited to cool off before speaking again. And by then there was no need for it.

Kyle had come up now. He still held his air of pretended courtesy.

"Don't play your sixty seconds too close, Soogan," he said, "but there's one thing I would like to have you think about. Jarvis has tried to blame the Carne boys for the cattle steal. He has intimated I am involved. Can you think of a better way for a thief to shift suspicion from himself than to place it on somebody else?"

"It's a good trick," Mack said, "and one that you use right well."

CHAPTER 14

The Clue That Pointed Nowhere

Up the road which hung like a taut ribbon along the side of the cliff Mack rode his sorrel, his own back a high, broad target. When he was through the gate he stopped, and waited for Gordon and Wade.

He watched Kyle return to the house. A moment later Dan Carne started up the road to the gate. Pete Carne and four other men moved toward the barn. Pete and one of his companions stopped to tinker with the mowers, but the other three went into the barn.

"Come on!" Natty Gordon said as he rode through the gate. "I kind of feel like I had a few coals of fire in my pocket."

They headed south toward the county road.

"Natty," Mack said, "you showed more nerve than I thought you had."

"Thanks." The deputy glowed. "But just the same I'm plumb glad to get out of there with a whole hide instead of a hole in my hide. I'd kind of like to go back down there sometime, though. There was a smell about the layout I didn't like."

"Hogwash!" Wade bellowed. "Fool hogwash! I didn't think you'd believe that stuff, Natty." He pointed a gnarled finger at Mack. "It gets too thick for me to swaller when you try to say Lou Kyle stole my beef. He's goin' to be my son-in-law. Does it make sense for him to rob me?"

"He ain't in your family yet, Soogan," Mack reminded. "A lot of things might happen."

"They will if you can make 'em happen!" Wade raged. "George Queen thinks you and Hinton stole my cows, and now Kyle's got the same notion. I never took no stock in it, but it looks now like there might be somethin' to it." He shook a fist under Mack's nose. "I ain't payin' you no five hundred dollars, cows or no cows, and yuh better tell Hinton to vamoose pronto. I ain't giving him till fall!"

"I never knew you to break a promise, Soogan," Mack said softly.

"And if I get any kind of proof on you," Wade raged on, "Natty's goin' to shove yuh into the calaboose!" He wheeled his horse, and put him into a dead run through the sagebrush.

"Reckon he don't like our company," Mack said.

Natty Gordon said nothing. Mack, glancing at him, saw that his face was hard and forbidding. The one moment in which he had shown some friendliness and belief that there might be something wrong in the Cove was gone. Natty Gordon would side against Kyle if he could gain favor with Soogan Wade. But he was too much of a politician to buck both of them.

They rode in silence to the county road and made the turn toward Axhandle, Gordon staring ahead at the twin ruts that ran their twisting course through the sagebrush.

"All right, Natty," Mack said heavily. "You're nothing but a two-bit, chiseling politician after all. You wouldn't have the courage to arrest Lou Kyle if you saw him committing ten crimes at once."

"You'll be in jail before Lou will," Gordon said darkly.

Natty Gordon put his horse into a gallop, reached the rim and dipped over it.

Mack Jarvis, riding slowly, watched the dust Gordon had

raised drift away from the road and add its gray to the sagebrush and felt the bitter stab of disappointment. He had
learned little of value, he had added to Natty Gordon's hatred
of him, and Kyle's subtle accusation had raised a doubt in
Wade's mind. It would have been better, he thought sourly,
if he had done anything else than what he had done this
day. . . .

The sun lay bright and hot upon Axhandle when Mack left
his sorrel in the stable, and strode rapidly to the feed store.

"Dad," he said, "I'm going to take a swing into the West
Sundowns to get this buyers' association rolling. It'll take me
a week. Mebbe more. Soon as I hit town, you'll head for
The Dalles."

"You don't have no real hopes about this buyers' association, do yuh, son?" asked Dad. "It won't be no more'n a
yellow-jacket buzzin' in Kyle's ears."

"A yellow-jacket can be plumb annoying, Dad. Get several of 'em working on Kyle, and mebbe he'll slap himself
silly."

Perrod gave Mack a cool, studying look.

"Yuh find out anything in the Cove?"

"Just got a hunch. Keep an eye on Kyle's butcher shop
while I'm gone. Count the steers they bring in, and get some
idea how much beef goes to the railroad camps."

There was a steady throb of restless energy in Mack that
brought him along the street from the feed store building to
the Mercantile and around the corner. In the back of the
block behind the warehouse were the buildings Kyle used for
a slaughterhouse and icehouse. They were too small, Mack
thought, for the amount of butchering that would be necessary to keep the railroad construction camps supplied, so
there would have to be continuous butchering and hauling
from Axhandle.

Mack stepped up on the loading platform of Kyle's warehouse, but he didn't go in. A man came out of the gloom of
the big building's interior, saw Mack and gave a short shrill

whistle. He jerked up a Winchester that had been leaning against the wall and stood watching Mack warily.

Almost immediately a second man came out of the warehouse, a rifle cradled in his arms. "Get out of here, Jarvis!" he said sharply. "No admittance to anybody not employed here, and especially you."

"I'm not trying to rob the place," Mack said irritably.

"Mebbe not, but you ain't comin' no closer. Boss' orders."

"This the way Kyle always runs a business?"

"He just give us the order a little over a week ago. Now you going to go, or do yuh figger on makin' trouble?"

"I guess there's nothin' around here that concerns me," Mack said indifferently and walked away.

The parts of the puzzle were here, Mack thought as he turned toward Inky Blair's printshop, all but one piece, and because that one piece was missing, the parts would not fall into place.

Inky was setting type when Mack came in. He swung around and, wiping a hand across his forehead, came to the desk.

"Find anything?"

"Tash Terris is in the Cove." Mack told him what had happened, and added, "Practically a wasted trip."

Inky grinned. "Mister, sounds like you've had quite a day."

Mack reached for a cigar. "These are free, I reckon?"

"Sure." Inky waved a ponderous hand. "Free to gents who are long on nerve and short on savvy."

"That part about being short on savvy is shore me." Mack slipped the cigar into his mouth, and began pacing the floor. "It's all there, Inky. Everything I need, but by the Eternal, I can't lay my hands on it."

"Keep working on it, and you'll wind up dead," Inky said somberly.

"Dan Carne was ready to let us have it, but Kyle was smarter. He figgered that once we'd had our look, and hadn't found anything, I'd never get Gordon and Soogan down there again." Mack came back to the desk. "Soogan's cows are down there in the Cove. I'd bet on it, but I couldn't see 'em and I couldn't see where they'd hide 'em. I've got a hunch it's Tomahawk beef Kyle's selling to the railroad, but how in time is he doing it?"

"I never was good on puzzles," Inky grunted.

"And another thing. Why is Kyle having the Carnes haul their hay into town? Why don't it go right out to the camps?"

"I don't know about that, but I did hear that Kyle was getting some horse feed down on the Columbia, and taking it to the camps."

"Something funny about that Carne hay," Mack said thoughtfully. "Got those order blanks ready?"

Inky moved to the back of the printshop and returned with a bundle.

"Here you are, friend. Heading out in the morning?"

"This afternoon."

"A lot of nice spots in the Sundowns for drygulching."

"I've got a nose for 'em," Mack said, and left the printshop.

He cruised along the boardwalk to the restaurant, saw Natty Gordon come out of the Casino and immediately go back, felt the hostility of the town.

"There goes a tough hand we could do without," he heard a man say.

Instinctively, Mack glanced toward the window of Rosella's hotel room, and wondered if she had gone. The thought of her brought a poignant stab to him, and he tried to put her from his mind. Still she lingered there, casting a dark shadow across his already dark mood.

He found the restaurant empty and took a middle stool. Betty, feeling the black run of his thoughts, waited in silence until he gave his order.

There was no satisfaction in the meal, and when Mack had finished his pie and drained his second cup of coffee, he still felt an emptiness in him that no amount of food would ever fill. He looked at Betty, tried to grin, and failed.

"Not much fun in life lately, Betty," he said. "Mebbe

we're working too hard, you filling men's stomachs and me doing nothing.''

"Not much fun," Betty agreed. And the laughter that usually was in her brown eyes was missing.

"I'm going into the Sundowns," Mack said. "Ride part of the way with me. Lock the place up and let 'em starve."

"I have a woman helping me now," Betty said. "She can run it."

"I'll get your mare," Mack said and left the restaurant.

A load of hay was coming along the street. Dan Carne was driving the team. When he saw Mack, he drew his gun, and laid it across his lap. Mack moved away from the front of the restaurant, and stood with his back to an empty lot, his eyes on Carne.

When the wagon was opposite Mack, Carne pulled up. A sudden quiet had come to the street, a hush as people moved to windows, and watched.

"Make your play," Mack said coldly. "You've got a gun in your hand, and mine's in leather, but I'll bring you off that hay before we're done."

"If it hadn't been for Soogan Wade," Carne said darkly, "you'd be dead now. I didn't give a hoot about the star packer, but I didn't want to beef Kyle's daddy-in-law."

"He ain't a daddy-in-law yet."

Carne jeered a laugh. "He will be, mister. He sure will be, and me and Pete will be there to dance at the weddin', but you won't. Between now and then Pete and me will have a date with you."

"Today's a good day."

"Not today. I've got a hunch you're fool enough to come snoopin' around the Cove again, and when yuh do, that'll be the day."

Carne spoke to his team then, and it seemed to Mack as he watched the horses strain into their collars, that it was harder to start the wagon rolling again than it should have been.

"What you got in that wagon besides hay?" he called.

"Nothing but hay," Carne said ominously, and began cursing his horses.

Mack waited until the wagon made the turn to the warehouse. Then he got his sorrel from the stable, told the hostler to saddle Betty's mare, and rode after the wagon. It stood beside the platform, no one making any effort to unload it.

Carne had unhooked the team, and driven it away. Mack reined up, and studied the load for a moment, but he could see nothing unusual about it except that it was small. He swung down and, stooping, looked under the hay rack.

It was then that the same two men who had stopped him on the loading platform came around the wagon.

"Jarvis, I don't know why you're so bent on hangin' around here," one of them said and patted his rifle. "But if you keep it up, you're goin' to get some hot lead right in the brisket."

"I'm interested in hay," Mack drawled. "You know I used to be in the feed business."

"You won't be in no business if yuh don't get out of here and stay out," the man snarled.

"One thing I can't figure out. Never saw anything like it before." Mack pointed under the wagon to a steady dribble of water that had made a wet black streak along the ground. "There seems to be a crack in the bottom of the hayrack. You reckon Carne raises hay that rains?"

The two men looked at each other, consternation sweeping across their stubby faces. One of them swore and began to back away. The other raised his rifle and thumbed back the hammer.

"Don't tell Natty Gordon what you saw," he said darkly, "or I'll hunt yuh to perdition and back. That hay's sweatin'. That's all. Just sweatin'. Savvy?"

"Yeah, I savvy," Mack said as he walked back to his horse. "Sure is hard-working hay."

Mack mounted and, riding back to the stable, got Betty's mare and led her to the restaurant. Betty came out, a shapely girl with still, unsmiling lips. Color was in her cheeks, but it seemed to Mack that she was wearing a cloak of sober dignity today that covered the sweetness and the laughter that usually were so much a part of her.

"It's been a long time since I was on a horse," she said. She stepped up, and reined her mount into the street. "Sometimes I wonder if the cost of making a living is worth it."

CHAPTER 15

Trouble in Trumpet

Betty was riding beside Mack as they turned toward the West Sundowns: rolling, pine-clad mountains that laid an irregular line along the horizon. They rode in silence until the town was behind them, Mack watching Betty and seeing the high way she held her head, the grace with which she rode.

"I never heard you talk like that before," he said, referring to her remark about the worth of making a living.

"I feel it more today," she said. "I'm thinking of selling the restaurant."

"You've made money, haven't you?"

"Money," Betty said bitterly. "Yes, I've made money, for all the good it is. I don't have a need for it like you do."

This was a side of her he had not seen before. He thought about it, the silence running on between them.

An hour later they had climbed a long ridge, and reached the first timber. Mack reined up.

"Mebbe you'd better start back," he suggested. "It'll be dark now before you get home."

"I need a stretch." Betty grimaced as she swung down. "I don't think I'll be able to sit much tomorrow."

Mack twisted a cigarette and held a match flame to it, feeling the change that was in the girl, neither understanding it nor knowing why it had come. Dismounting, he pointed south to where the rim-rock widened to make Pioneer Valley.

"There'll be a lot of people living there some day," he said. "Mebbe they'll look back on us and call us pioneers."

"Why don't they come now?"

"They're too soft. Somebody's got to tame a country."

"Where will you be when they come, Mack?"

"Why, I don't know. Tumbleweeds roll with the wind. Guess I'll be rolling again, with some wind to my back."

"And you'll carry the same toughness with you that's in you now. Mack, I've seen you change. You don't laugh like you did. The town has turned against you, and it's hurt you more than you have let yourself know."

Knowing that it was true, he did not argue.

"I reckon it's no good to count on something too much," he said instead. "Mebbe it's better to let the wind carry you."

"No, Mack," she said fiercely. "But when you've lost, there's no sense in letting your whole life be made bitter."

"Mebbe after Lou Kyle's dead, my life won't be bitter. It'd sure make the world a better place for a heap of people."

"I don't know about that," she said thoughtfully. "My folks were killed in the Piute-Bannock War, and I knew of some white men who killed their Indian prisoners. It didn't help, much. It didn't bring my folks back."

"That's different," Mack said indignantly.

"I know." She laid a hand on his arm. "You're fighting for a principle, but while you're fighting for that principle, you're becoming tough and hard. Don't change, Mack."

"This won't last forever," he assured her. "What's this about you selling out?"

"I don't know," she murmured. She moved away from him, her eyes on the valley, a deep hunger in her life she had never known. "I never had a home after my folks were killed, and it's the thing I've dreamed most about, but maybe it's one of these things that is never more than a dream."

Mack thought of Rosella and of his own dreams, and how

they had centered around her. It would have been better if he had never met her. If it had not been for an unkind fate, it would have been that way. But they had met; the longing for her was still in him, and to call himself a fool was no answer for it.

"It's a tough life, if you're going to take what it gives you," he said a little roughly. "I've always taken what I wanted. Mebbe I'll have what I want before this is over."

"Are you still sure you want it?"

Jimmy Hinton came to his mind then, and the question Jimmy had asked him. What would he do if Rosella saw her mistake in time, and decided she would rather have him than Lou Kyle?

He had told Jimmy he'd marry her at once, if she said so.

"I never try swimming a river till I get to it," he said now. He turned back to his sorrel and stepped up. "I've got to move. I want to get back into the timber before I camp."

"Be careful, Mack."

"I'll look behind every pine," he said. "And don't sell out too soon. Dad's cooking ain't so much after getting used to yours."

He grinned then, a wide-lipped, boyish grin that made him more like the old Mack Jarvis. He raised his Stetson, a courteous, gallant gesture that came without thought.

When he was deep in the timber and she was out of sight, he wondered idly if he had ever lifted his hat to Rosella. He could not remember that he ever had, but Lou Kyle had, and it would be one of the things Rosella would like. Kyle had ways that he did not. A man was what he was, though, and it was not in him to copy another.

Then his mind came back to Betty, and he asked himself what there had been about her that had brought that action from him. He searched himself, and found no answer. . . .

It took Mack a week to cover the Sundowns and the blackness grew in him each day. Always it was the same. These men who had been in the Casino and had first made the proposition now wanted no part of the buyers' association. They wouldn't look at Mack when they talked to him. They were jumpy and they were afraid. Kyle's long arm had reached from Axhandle here to the mountain wilderness.

The story was the same when Mack wangled it out of them. Jake Singleton, the big man of the town of Trumpet, had got to them ahead of Mack. By some miracle of communication Kyle had heard of the plan, and had sent word to Singleton in time. He had told them that Kyle would give them more time on their loans, they could have credit at the Mercantile—and there was always the carefully veiled threat of reprisals if they tried to do business with Mack.

"Mighty funny Kyle would get so bighearted overnight," Mack would observe.

After he had said that, they would start looking across the clearing into the timber, or build a smoke, or perhaps pick up a pine limb and begin whittling. Cowardice was in them, and because of it shame was there. All of them knew it and felt it and showed a brusqueness that was not like them.

"He's given us what we wanted," they would say, "and we'd have to pay you somethin' if we went ahead with this buyers' association." Then their eyes would meet Mack's, and fear would be a naked thing in them.

"Last year a man up on Bear Creek allowed he'd buck Kyle," one man had put it. "Claimed he'd set up a store and freight his own stuff in. One night he got plugged between the eyes and his place burned. We've got families, Jarvis. We can't take no chances on that happenin' to us."

"Sure," Mack would say. "I see how it is."

Mack never made camp in the same place twice, and he seldom followed the road. He kept his fires small, and he put them out as soon as he was done with them. He would sit quietly then, and smoke, and stare at the blue sky through a lacework of pine needles.

He would think about the problems that faced him and his mind would come to Dan Carne's load of hay and the dribble of water he had seen marking its line upon the ground. This made no sense at all, yet the feeling stayed in him that there was something important about it.

Eventually Mack's mind would turn to Jake Singleton, and as he came closer to the summit and closer to the town of Trumpet, the desire to see Singleton grew in him. That Singleton was Kyle's man was something Mack had not known before. It proved again, as it had been proved so many times to Mack, that there was no end to Lou Kyle's scheming, no end to his ambitions; that his legitimate businesses were cloaks to cover his lawless activities.

Trumpet belonged to Singleton. That much Mack knew. Just as he knew that Trumpet was a small settlement atop the Sundowns where a man could find a room and meals and drinks when the rest of the state was too hot for him.

Mack came to Trumpet in the evening of the sixth day after he had left Axhandle. It lay between two mountains, the trail snaking on past to drop downgrade and eventually reach the Columbia. There was not much to the town—a rambling structure that was hotel and saloon, with a log barn and corrals behind the large building, and a half dozen cabins scattered haphazardly along the trail beyond the hotel.

Twilight lay all about in the thick blueness and gave to the sprawling town that strange mystery which comes to the earth as day slides into night. The mountains on both sides of the settlement rose in round perfection, standing close together and pinching Trumpet into a long, narrow shape.

Racking his sorrel, Mack Jarvis went into the saloon. A crude pine bar ran half the length of the south side. Two rickety poker tables stood along the opposite wall. There were cobwebs and filth and a great smell of evil about the place.

Mack crossed the room, the floor boards squeaking under his weight. Seeing no one, he moved around the bar and through the door into the hotel lobby. The desk was no more than a crude pine table, and there was as much filth here as in the saloon. Two broken-backed chairs were set close to the front windows. In the gloom behind the desk a paunchy man sat with his chair tilted back against the wall, his mouth open, his snores steady, discordant, and wheezy.

Mack pushed a toe under the front leg of the man's chair, and lifted. The back legs scooted forward, and the paunchy man hit the floor on his back, hard, the lamp on the desk rattling with the fall. He swallowed a snore on the way down, choked, and rolled over.

"What the thunderation!" was jolted out of him.

Mack lighted the lamp, and blew out the match.

"It ain't dark yet," the paunchy man snarled. "No use wastin' coal oil!"

Mack flipped the still smoking match at the man. It hit his cheek, rolled on down his fat neck, and brought a squall out of him. He batted it away.

"Tough, eh?" he growled, and came to his feet, hand pulling a gun from a shoulder holster.

"Tough enough," Mack said, and hit the man on the side of the head.

The paunchy one sat down again, his gun falling out of his hand. He stared up at Mack.

"Mebbe you are tough, mister," he said. "Who the devil are yuh?"

"You Jake Singleton?"

"Yeah, I'm Singleton. I asked who you are."

"Mack Jarvis."

Singleton got up, jerked his chair upright, and sat down on it, his eyes covertly on Mack.

"Let's go have a drink," he said.

"I don't want your rotgut. I want information."

"Yeah?" Singleton laughed shortly. "I know plenty, friend, but most of what I know I couldn't tell. When yuh run a place like this yuh keep your lip buttoned."

"I want to know what your tieup with Kyle is," Mack cut in.

Singleton felt of his face where Mack had hit him. His nose was flat and red, his mouth wide and thick of lip, his eyes small and wicked.

"I figured that was what you wanted," he said. His lips came away from a single yellow tooth in a grin. "Fact is, Kyle said yuh'd show up here as soon as you found out who spiked your buyers' association. In a place like this a thousand dollars is a pile of dinero. He figures you're worth that to him dead. That's why you're headed for Boot Hill, mister. You are goin' to be—''

Mack sensed the play. He saw Singleton's eyes flick away from him toward the front door, felt the stiffening expectancy in the man, and the knowledge that death had come into the room ran a chill along his spine. He came around fast, pulling gun as he turned, and dove sideward as he glimpsed the two men who had come in.

A bullet splintered the door casing. Another breathed sharply along his cheek and slapped into the wall behind him. Then Mack had the men targeted, sent one of them into a lurching fall with a bullet in his chest, and smashed the second one's right arm. The gunman cursed shrilly, stooped, and reached with his left hand for the Colt he had dropped.

"Pick it up and I'll kill you," Mack said coldly.

The gunman straightened, right arm dangling, and began to curse again.

"I ought to kill you, Singleton," Mack grated.

Singleton got up, and stepped around the table, watching Mack closely.

"I couldn't see why one man could spook Kyle like you have," he said, "but now that I've seen yuh, I know."

"How's Kyle gettin' Tomahawk beef out of Carne Cove?" Mack demanded.

Singleton shook his head. "Blamed if I know, friend. I don't have no worries about that end. I've got a workin' agreement with him to find a good man when he wants a killing done, but I sure missed this time."

"The next miss will be your end," Mack said grimly. "I don't know what keeps me from killing you right now."

"I don't intend to do you no harm," Singleton said, fear in his eyes. "I'm ready to call it quits."

"What makes you think I'll believe it?" Mack asked, "after what just happened here? Give you half a chance and you'll be ready to lift my scalp again. I know your type."

"I'm through with Kyle," Singleton said.

"Mebbe," Mack allowed. "But Kyle can have you back any time he wants."

Singleton looked at the dead and the injured gunmen. "They can be my witnesses," he said.

"You've got to fix my arm, Singleton!" the wounded man whimpered.

Outside, the run of a horse on the trail came to Mack clearly. He listened a moment, saw hope break across Singleton's face.

"I'm going into the other room," he said. "Watch your tongue, Singleton. If I get more trouble, you'll have a chunk of it."

"I savvy."

CHAPTER 16

Death on Tomahawk Range

Darting to the door, Mack slid into the dining room and took up a listening post. He heard a man walk across the lobby.

"Howdy," he heard Singleton say.

"Who killed this man?" The voice was Natty Gordon's.

"Mack Jarvis," Singleton mumbled.

There was a pause then, and Mack, watching through a crack in the door, saw Gordon scratch his cheek and stare at the dead man as if he could not make up his mind whether he wanted to stay or not.

"Quite a ride from Axhandle just to ask about a dead man, ain't it?" Singleton asked.

"Yeah. Quite a ride. Is Mack around?"

"He's around. Yuh want him?"

Gordon swallowed, looked at the dead man again.

"Yeah," he said, "that's why I'm here. He's wanted in Axhandle for stealing Tomahawk beef. We found a pile of Tomahawk hides in the back room of his feed store."

A club blow to Mack's middle would have had nearly the same effect as Natty's words. It was crazy, this latest play by

Kyle. Sane men would see through it, but Axhandle people weren't exactly sane when Lou Kyle was calling the turn. What was more, he could pull enough wires, even with planted evidence like this, to send Mack to the Salem pen.

Mack, thinking swiftly of this, eased out of the dining room and through the kitchen. He came around the building and stepped into the lobby. "So you're looking for me, are yuh, Natty?" he said softly.

The expression on the deputy's face showed the quick fear that raced through him. He swallowed hard.

"You're under arrest, Mack!" he said shrilly. "Unbuckle your gunbelt."

"If you want me, come after me," Mack taunted.

"Don't resist arrest!" Gordon cried. "You'll make it harder for yourself."

"Natty," Mack said, "you're so anxious to hang onto your job that you've shoved whatever common sense you had plumb out of your brain. You know that if I had stole Tomahawk beef, I wouldn't be fool enough to leave a bunch of hides in my back room."

"You fizzled out on your store," Natty said, "and I'm not crazy enough to think you'd pass up a chance to make a few dollars."

"You're crazy if you do believe it."

"Mack, I'm not the one who tries you," Gordon pleaded. "The smart thing for you to do is to come along without makin' trouble and stand trial."

Mack shook his head. "You know I wouldn't stand the chance of a snowflake in the hot place. But I'm going back down into the Cove, and when I find out how this steal is being worked I'll get you, and you'll have a chance to use that star for the purpose it's supposed to be used for."

"I'm not goin' down there again," Gordon said flatly.

Mack grinned sardonically. "You'll go, Natty. Now ride back to Kyle and tell him not to send a boy to do a man's chores next time." He saw temper build in Gordon, and added, "Take it easy, Natty, and don't try followin' me."

Mack went out of the door in a quick, sideward movement, and hit the saddle as he heard the wounded man's shrill cry:

"I've got to have this arm fixed, Singleton!"

Mack fired two quick shots into the front of the hotel, and put his horse into a run. A moment later the forest darkness had hidden him.

He rode until dawn, then went down a canyon to his right, and made camp. He slept most of the day, and when he went on he kept off the trail, reining up occasionally and letting his ears keen the wind for the sound of pursuit. He was any man's target now, and for that reason he moved with greater caution than was his habit.

It was dark by the time Mack reached the rim and came warily down the narrow road and on into Axhandle. Leaving his sorrel in the willows alongside the creek, he followed the littered alley to the back of his feed store building. He tried the door, but it was locked.

He knocked, stepped away from the door, and when it opened, he said softly:

"Blow the light out till I get inside."

Apparently Perrod didn't hear.

"Cuss them dogs!" he said loudly, and went back.

Mack waited and, hearing no sound of movement, carefully opened the door and slid in.

"Better not show a light," Perrod cautioned.

"Got anything to eat?"

"I can rustle yuh some cold meat and biscuits. Got some coffee on the stove that ain't real hot . . . How'd yuh hear?"

"Natty set out to get me," Mack answered. "Is he back yet?"

"Ain't seen him. Him and Kyle had quite a ruckus in the Casino the other night, and Kyle allowed Natty wasn't much of a lawman. Reckon Natty thought if he brought you in, he'd be standin' in pretty good with Kyle."

"What happened here?" Mack asked, while he ate. "Natty claimed he found some hides."

"He found 'em all right," Perrod said. "In that danged store-room. I ain't looked there since we cleaned everything out the other day. Some of them polecats must of come in and left them hides there when I wasn't around. Anyhow, when Gordon showed up saying he wanted a look, I didn't make him no trouble.''

"How many did he find?"

"Four. Hadn't come off the cows long, neither."

"Fix up a sack of grub, Dad," Mack said, "I'm riding out to Jimmy Hinton's."

Mack twisted a smoke, cupping a hand over the match flame when he lighted it, and by the time he had finished the cigarette, Perrod laid a sack of food on his lap.

"What did you learn about Kyle's butcherin'?" Mack asked.

"He's haulin' about fifteen beefs a day to the camps, near as I could tell," Perrod said. "He ain't butchered that many by a danged sight. George Queen drove in one bunch the other day. About twenty-five head, and that's all Kyle's bought on the hoof.''

"Even a stubborn gent like Soogan could see what's going on," Mack said hotly.

"No, don't reckon he would. Them meat wagons go out in the night. Nothin' funny about it, because that way he gets the meat to the camps early in the mornin'. Wouldn't have it out in the sun."

Mack moved to the door. "Keep your eyes peeled, Dad."

"Wait a minute, son. There was some graders in from one of the camps, and they was worked up about the meat they was gettin'. Claimed some of the boys got sick from eatin' it, like mebbe it was spoiled. They was all set to quit till their boss told 'em they'd get good meat, and might even have some pork before long."

Jimmy Hinton had the only large number of hogs anywhere along Pioneer Creek. That thought came first to Mack, and hard upon it was the second thought that if the Carnes would steel beef from Soogan Wade, they would steal pork from Jimmy Hinton.

"So long, Dad," he said, and opened the door and slid out into the night.

Mack made a swing around the town, and took the high desert road. He came again past the Carne gate, circling away from the road into the sage so he would not be seen if a guard was posted there. He went on toward Round Butte, and came again to the lava flow, the wildness of the black, twisted mass adding to the turbulence in his mind.

There was no light in the window of Jimmy Hinton's cabin! It was late, yet Mack was remembering it had been late the last time he was here, and Jimmy had been reading.

Mack pulled up before he came out of the sage, and sat motionless for a time, the cabin bulking darkly before him, trouble making a strong smell in his nostrils. He stepped down, and moved catlike toward the cabin.

Again Mack paused before he came into the yard, plucked gun, and stood with his ears keening the slow breeze for stray sounds, eyes strained to catch any movement that would break the stillness. There was none, yet the smell of trouble remained as if death had come and let its black wings cease their fluttering while it kept its vigil, a somber thing between life and eternity.

He came through the gate, stiffly and slowly, as a man frozen. He was almost to the cabin when he saw the shapeless black form on the ground, and what he had feared became a certainty. He struck a match and held it to the man's face. The dead man was Metolius Neele.

The flame traveled along the match, touched his fingers, and burned while his mind took cognizance of this thing he had seen, and could not fully grasp. Neele had been shot in the chest. His gun was still in his holster.

"Jimmy didn't kill him," Mack thought. "Jimmy couldn't kill any human being."

Mack rose and called softly, "Jimmy!"

There was only silence that ran on and on mockingly, a still night without sound except for the coyote calls from the Sundowns. He went on into the cabin, boot heels cracking pistol-like on the boards. He brought another match to life, and lighted the lamp on the table.

Then his eyes were on it, back in the shadows alongside the bunks. Jimmy Hinton's body was there, twisted and still, and when Mack put a hand on the wrist, he found that it was cold.

There was no emotion and no thought in Mack Jarvis then. He had felt that this would happen when he had left Jimmy the last time. He knelt beside the body, and words came out of his mouth without conscious direction.

"The dirty, killing sons! The dirty, killing sons!" Then he was aware that he was speaking, his voice sounding far-away and strange to his ears, and he stopped.

Jimmy Hinton was lying on his side, right hand under him. Mack turned him over. In his hand was a gold coin with two small holes bored through it, the kind of a button Soogan Wade wore on his coat.

The moments ran on, uncounted, while Mack stared at the gold button, and presently his mind focused clearly upon it. There could be but one explanation. Soogan Wade had shot Jimmy, and in his excitement had not known that Jimmy had flung out a hand and jerked the coin from Wade's coat as he had fallen.

Mack pulled Neele's body into the house and shut the door. Then he mounted and rode south toward Tomahawk. Wade would be there, or in town. In either case, he was going to jail, and Natty Gordon, politician that he was, could not overlook a clue like the gold coin button.

Mack rode until after midnight, a single thought nagging steadily at his brain. Jimmy Hinton was dead, and his going had left a great emptiness in Mack that no one else would ever fill.

"It's everybody's fight," Hinton had said. "It's going on all over the world. It's humanity against evil. This is just a skirmish, but you've got to win it."

With only the glow of the stars above him, Mack swore to himself he would win this skirmish, and part of winning it was to bring Jimmy Hinton's murderer to a hangman's rope.

When he came at last to the Tomahawk buildings, Mack paused, searching for a light, and seeing none. Quiet was all about. It was familiar ground, and it struck him that it took a perverse fate to deal him this kind of a hand, to bring him on so grim an errand to the ranch where he had met Rosella.

CHAPTER 17

Charge and Counter-Charge

Leaving his sorrel in a dry wash south of the house, Mack moved swiftly toward it and through the locust trees in front. A dog scurried around the corner of the house, barking shrilly, but stopped when Mack said, "All right, Nip."

He stepped across the porch, the screech of boards under his feet terrifyingly loud, and went on into the house.

Mack shut the door, dropped the bar, and paused to get his bearings. It was a log structure with a huge living room that ran the full width of the house except for a small corner which had been partitioned off to serve as an office.

Soogan's bedroom was in the back of the house, but he often slept on a couch in the office when he worked late. Mack moved toward it, wanting a look before he went on to the back. He slid into the office, struck a match, and lighted a lamp. Soogan was on the couch, a tattered quilt thrown over him.

Mack pulled his gun just as the old man threw back his quilt.

"What the devil are you up to, Mack?" he roared.

He swung his bare feet to the floor and sat up. He knuckled

his eyes, shook his head, and slowly became aware of what was happening. He pointed at the gun in Mack's hand.

"What's that for, you damned fool?" he bellowed.

Wade made a comical figure in his underwear, gray hair awry, long, bony feet on the floor, his huge, untrimmed mustache drooping sadly around his mouth. Even his eyes were not as bright and sharp as usual, and the belligerent aggressiveness that had always dominated the old cowman was not in him now.

"Soogan, you've been tough and ornery in your days," Mack said coldly, "but I never thought you'd cold turkey a man like you did Jimmy Hinton."

Blankness came over Wade's lined face as his mind groped for the meaning of Mack's words. Then he said:

"Son, I don't know what you're talking about."

"You killed Jimmy, and I'm taking you into town."

"Put that iron up," Wade said testily. "I didn't beef Hinton."

Mack picked Wade's coat up from a chair, and pointed to where frayed threads had once held a button.

"Look at that, Soogan, and then look at what I found in Jimmy's hand. He'd been shot up close, and I reckon he grabbed this as he went down."

Wade looked at the coat, then at the coin button, and raised his eyes to Mack.

"Son," he said, "you and me have been on different sides for quite a spell now, but no matter what's happened, I've never lied to you. I didn't kill Jimmy Hinton."

"What about this button?" Mack demanded.

"All I know is that I lost it several days ago. Last time I remember seein' it was when I was standin' at the bar in the Casino drinking with Lou. I got pretty drunk. Mebbe I pulled it off myself. I sure can't remember."

"I never saw you drunk, Soogan."

"Well, me and Lou got to gabbin' about Rosella and the ranch. I guess I just forgot to stop."

"Mebbe Kyle kept pushing 'em at you?"

"Yeah, he did. Wanted to celebrate." Wade paused, an

angry frown lining his forehead. "What you gettin' at, Mack?"

"I was thinking mebbe Kyle pulled that button off to frame you."

"I thought mebbe Kyle was gettin' around to that!" Wade bellowed angrily. "I'm rememberin' they found some Tomahawk hides in your storeroom, Mack. I didn't take no stock in it, but when you get so cussed anxious to pile this on Lou, I'm thinkin' I better believe it about them hides!"

"You're too smart to believe planted evidence like that," Mack said thoughtfully, "and I should have known better than to believe you beefed Jimmy. It begins to shape up now. I couldn't figger out about Metolius."

"What about Metolius?" Wade demanded.

Mack told him what had happened.

"Looks like Kyle and the Carne boys to me," he added.

"Metolius—dead!" Wade pointed a trembling finger at Mack. "You salivated him! Metolius got the goods on you, caught up with you when you was there at Hinton's and he got Hinton while you plugged *him*. That's about the way it was!"

"You're thinking just what Kyle wants you to think. Use your head, Soogan."

"I'm using it!" Wade raged. "If Natty Gordon never done anything in his life before, he's goin' to do something now. You've got more'n a cow-stealing charge against you. You're goin' to hang for killing Metolius Neele!"

Wade got up, but sat down again as Mack pronged back the hammer of his gun.

"Soogan," he said, "there's no evidence to hook me up with shooting Metolius, but this button is something you can't argue yourself out of. Now get on your pants, and let's ride."

"Drop your gun, Mack!"

Rosella stood in the doorway behind Mack, a small pistol in her hand.

Outside George Queen raised a great voice.

"What's goin' on, Soogan? Any trouble?"

"Mack Jarvis is in here!" Wade thundered. "Smoke him out!"

"It'll be a pleasure, Soogan!" Queen yelled.

Mack heard the run of feet toward the front door, and a pounding against it. He was trapped.

The odds against him were ten to one, and George Queen would welcome the task that Wade had given him.

Mack did not let his gun go. He turned so that he could see Rosella and still watch Wade.

"I didn't come here to hurt Soogan," he said, "but if you squeeze that trigger, Rosella, he'll get hurt."

Rosella had not lost her poise, but Mack knew she was thinking, and that her conclusion would mean his life. Her eyes flicked once to the front door and came back to him. Her lips were tightly pressed together.

"Drill him, girl!" Wade howled. "Cuss it, go ahead and drill him!"

Outside George Queen was pounding on the door.

"Open up!" he was bellowing.

"They'll kill you." Rosella jerked her head toward the door.

"Might be." Mack agreed.

"I can't shoot him like this, Dad. Come on, Mack."

"I'm pulling out, George!" Mack called, and put two quick shots through the top of the door. "Don't try coming after me."

"Come on," Rosella said again, and led Mack through the living room and into the hall behind it. "In here." She opened a door and shoved Mack through.

Soogan Wade lifted the bar to the front door.

"He got out the back, George."

Mack heard the tramp of Queen and his men along the hall and into the kitchen. There was silence for a time, then Queen asked:

"What'd he want you for, Soogan?"

"He was fixin' to take me to town for killing Jimmy Hinton. Metolius was shot, too."

"Metolius?" Queen asked incredulously. "You're sure?"

"That's what Mack said."

"We'll go fetch the body," Queen said heavily. "Looks like Mack got his hoss and pulled out. Chances are we'll pick him up around Hinton's cabin. I'll leave a few of the boys here in case he's hiding."

Rosella slid into the room where she had left Mack.

"What happened?" she whispered.

Mack told her, and before he had finished, he heard the thunder of hoofs as the Tomahawk men left the yard.

She was standing close to him in the darkness, the fragrance of her hair in his nostrils. The old hunger for her was sweeping over him. He reached for her, put his arms around her, and she came to him willingly.

"Mack, will you ever understand?" she whispered.

"I think I do," he said roughly, and let her go. For a moment he had forgotten. "You made a deal and I'm hoping it'll make you happy."

"I'll keep the deal I made, but if a man once loved a girl—"

"He goes on loving her, and makes a fool out of himself because of it."

"I hate you!" she flung at him.

"Mebbe we'd both feel better if we start hating each other."

"Wait, Mack!" She caught his arm as he moved toward the door. "What was that talk about Lou using Dad's button to frame him?"

"I can't prove it. I'd better drift."

"Mack, why should Lou want to frame Dad for anything?"

"If Soogan was dead," Mack said bluntly, "Kyle would talk you into marrying him pronto. Then he'd be fixed with a mighty fine ranch."

"But he's got money, Mack."

"Mebbe," he said, and let it go at that. "Thanks for saving my hide."

Mack stepped into the hall and catfooted along it into the living room. He saw that it was empty and, moving through it to the front door, went across the porch and yard on the run. Somebody from the side of the house heard him, glimpsed his shadowy figure, and opened up with a .45.

Mack raced through the locust trees, felt the breath of a slug, and triggered three shots at the man who was firing. He ran on, angling sharply to his left, and reached his sorrel.

"You let him get away, you fools!" he heard Wade's hoarse bellow. "Get your horses! Bust the breeze after him!"

Mack smiled grimly as he stepped into saddle and swung his sorrel in a wide circle away from the house. Soogan Wade was a man in whom anger rose high and soon fell away. Later he would be glad that Mack had not died at his order.

It was early morning when Mack rode into Hinton's yard. The Tomahawk men had taken Metolius Neele's body, but Hinton was still where Mack had left it. Mack buried his friend behind the cabin, and placed a cross at the head of the grave. Finding a Bible among Hinton's books, Mack read aloud the Twenty-Third Psalm, haltingly, feeling the power and promise of those lines.

Then he looked up at the sky, and it was as if he were looking far beyond that blue bowl into the endless expanse of eternity.

"God, I ain't fit to be talking to you," he said, "but there's nobody else around. I know you'll look out for Jimmy because he was a fine man, and I reckon you can answer all the questions he couldn't get answered down here. Amen."

Hinton's hogs were gone, but his horse was still in the barn. Mack turned the animal loose and taking a pair of binoculars from the cabin, rode away. The need of haste was pressing him, for he knew that Queen and his men would come again to look for him.

He made a half-circle of Round Butte, and put his sorrel up the cinder slope in easy switchbacks. Leaving his horse in the cup-like crater, he climbed the inside slope to the top above Hinton's cabin, and looked down.

A half-dozen Tomahawk men were sitting their saddles between the barn and the cabin, and when Mack studied them through the glasses, he saw the puzzled expressions on their

faces. Queen was talking to them, and presently three took
the road to town while Queen and the others started back to
Tomahawk.

Mack circled to the opposite side of the crater, and spent
the rest of the day studying the lava flow that twisted below
him like a motionless, gray-black snake. The desert was spread
before him in a far-flung panorama of sage and junipers, and
to the north and east were the pine-covered Sundowns.

He wasn't sure what to expect, but he believed that a pe-
riod of consistent watching would turn up a vital clue. The
lava flow formed a terrain over which cattle could be driven
without leaving tracks, and if there was a secret entrance into
the Cove, the lava might be the avenue which the cattle had
traveled.

For a long time Mack lay studying it, noting the ten-foot
wall which it formed along the lip of the canyon. It was the
wall which made Mack wonder if there was any sense in
continuing his watch. Even if cattle had been driven across
the lava, and had followed the long, spine-like ridges which
Mack had seen when he was in the Cove, they couldn't climb
a ten-foot wall.

A feeling of desperation ran along Mack's tense nerves.
All the evidence he had pointed to the one conclusion that
the Cove was the hiding place for Tomahawk cattle, yet the
facts consistently denied that same conclusion. Apparently
Kyle and the Carnes were taking no chances, for their scheme,
whatever it was, seemed above detection.

CHAPTER 18

Secret of the Cove

Early dark fell at last, and Mack rode back to the cabin, watered his sorrel, and fed him. He barred the door of the cabin and hung blankets over the windows before he lighted a lamp. Then he cooked supper, ate, and spent several minutes finding the trap door that opened into the narrow cave below the cabin.

There was no money, but there was a metal box containing a key and a letter to him. He read:

Dear Mack,

My money is in a box in the Axhandle bank. Remember you are to use it as you need it. You will not be reading this unless I am dead, and that may be soon because I am going into the Cove tomorrow to continue my investigation. I have found out that the cattle were taken from the range through the lava wall—

The brittle sound of breaking window glass brought Mack out of his chair. He drew gun as he turned, but there was no time to fire. A hand jerked the blanket from the window, and a gun flamed, the bullet lashing across the top of his head and driving consciousness from him. . . .

A cold wind blowing into the cabin through an open door and shattered window brought Mack back to an aching consciousness. Memory came to him slowly, and with it was the feeling that after he had been shot he had heard more firing and the hoofbeats of running horses. He pulled himself into his chair and saw that both the key and Jimmy's letter were gone.

"Mack, are you all right?"

Betty Grant was standing in the doorway, looking worried, and holding herself under a high tension. She was wearing her riding outfit, and there was a gun on her hip. That was the picture Mack caught, and he told himself he must be out of his head.

"Mack, are you hurt!"

She came to him swiftly, her cool fingers examining his wound. She shut the door, plugged the broken window with a wad of blankets, and built up the fire. Presently she brought a pan of hot water to the table, washed the wound, and bandaged it.

"How do you happen to turn up here?" he asked.

"Mostly because I was worried about you."

Mark twisted a cigarette, his eyes on the girl, seeing the sheen the lamplight put upon her dark hair and sensing the sweetness and courage that was in her. It had always been Rosella in his thought; the things she had said and done had not changed that. Love had meant that to him, a tight and unchangeable power holding a man and lasting as long as life itself.

Now, with Betty here before him, he felt the strength and steadiness of her character, saw the beauty that it gave her.

"Why were you worried?" he asked.

"Tomahawk men are in town looking for you."

"I've got a little business to settle with the Carne boys and Kyle before I show up in town," he said grimly. "I thought I heard some more shooting outside. Did I dream it?"

"No. I wasn't far from the cabin when I heard the shot

and saw the light in the window. Another man was on a horse close to the porch. I circled into the sagebrush and started firing. The man who shot you had climbed in through the window, and when he heard me he came out through the door, jumped into saddle, and they both lit out.''

"Wonder who that hombre could have been?"

"Looked like Kyle, but I couldn't be sure." Betty came to him, and laid a hand on his arm. "Mack, you can't go on fighting alone this way."

"I've got some help from people I didn't figure on." He glanced at his watch. "It's quite a while till daylight. Now that you're on vacation, mebbe you'd like to cook."

She smiled. "Of course."

They left the cabin before dawn, and by the time morning grayness was flowing across the earth, they were inside Round Butte's crater, their eyes on the lava wall rising above the east rim.

"Light ain't real good yet," Mack said, as he drew the binoculars from the case. He stared at the rock wall, looked through the glasses and lowered them again. "Betty, am I seeing things, or is that a notch in that wall over there?"

Betty studied the wall for a time.

"It's a notch all right," she said then. "Looks like a V, but I don't see anything about it to get worked up over."

"Just that it wasn't there yesterday. That's all."

They waited for a time, eyes fixed on the notch, and presently Mack looked through the glasses again. What he saw brought an exclamation from him. A man was lifting a huge boulder and carrying it toward the notch. Mack handed the glasses to Betty.

"Take a look."

Betty had her look, took the glasses from her eyes, and shook her head.

"Mack, I've just seen something that couldn't have happened. See if you can find the notch."

She gave the glasses back.

Mack looked for a long moment, moving his glasses so that he brought the entire length of the wall into his vision.

"It isn't there," he said in awe.

"First, I saw a man carrying a boulder which was too big for him to handle if the law of gravity is still in force."

"What happened to the notch?" Mack demanded.

"He plugged it with that boulder."

"I'm going down to take a close look." Mack stood up and slipped the glasses into the case. "You'd better light out for town."

"No," Betty said flatly. "Not till I find out what's going on."

They rode down the east slope of the butte and followed the lava flow until they reached the spot where they had seen the notch. Betty watched in silence while Mack made a careful examination of the lava wall. It was midmorning before he whistled softly, and stepped back from the lava to view it at a greater distance.

"Pretty smart," he said softly. "If we hadn't spotted that jigger through the glasses, we'd have hunted all summer and not found this."

"Looks like lava rock to me," Betty said skeptically.

"Which is what they wanted us to think. Looks to me like they lift this out at night and put it back about dawn. Some time during the night they chouse a few cows through, or mebbe the critters drift through."

"Will you tell me what you're talking about?" Betty demanded.

"Rub your hand along this chunk of lava, and then on over here."

Betty obeyed, and wheeled to face Mac.

"It's soft here. It's . . . Mac, it's pumice!" She turned back, fingers searching for the edge of the pumice plug. "I'll bet I could lift that thing myself."

"You could hoist that chunk all right, but don't do it."

"Why not?"

"I have an idea Jimmy pulled it out, and got drilled for his trouble." He looked at her for a moment as if deciding his own course of action, then said, "There's one chore you could do for me."

"What is it?"

"Tell Natty Gordon I'll give myself up if he'll ride out here alone. Tell him I'll be at Round Butte this evening."

"I hope you know what you're doing," she said doubtfully. Stepping into saddle, she sat for a moment staring at the pumice. "How did they get that pumice to look as dark as lava?"

"I wondered about that." Mack ran his hand over the pumice. "They've rubbed something on it. Charcoal, or soot."

"Great idea," Betty said. She smiled at Mack and rode away. . . .

Mack was waiting atop a lava upthrust that evening when he saw Natty Gordon approaching. The deputy was riding slowly, a Winchester carried across his saddle.

"Pull up, Natty," Mack called, "and don't make a fast move."

"You told Betty you'd give yourself up," Gordon said sourly.

"I aim to," Mack said, "but I ain't going back to town as long as Lou Kyle holds the whiphand like he does."

"You've got to stand trial," Gordon said doggedly.

"I don't think so. Let's face our cards. You're a politician wanting to hold your job. I aim to get clear of these trumped-up charges you've got against me. Let's work together, Natty."

Gordon scratched a cheek a moment.

"Soogan—" he began.

"Soogan's our man," Mack cut in. "Tonight you and me are going to prove it's Kyle who stole his beef. Then he'll listen. In the long run, Natty, you'll be standing ace high with everybody.It ain't often a deputy sheriff can bring a crook the size of Kyle off his throne."

For a long time Gordon stared at the bronze blob that was Mack's face.

"All right, Mack," he said finally. "It's a bargain."

Quickly Mack sketched what had happened, and added,

"Looks to me like the Carnes did the stealing and Kyle had the market."

"Might be," Gordon admitted. "While you've been gone, Inky Blair wrote to the Pioneer Valley Railroad Company about Bishop giving both contracts to Kyle without nobody else having a chance. The upshot of it was the company sent their chief special agent to Axhandle to do a little nosin' around."

"It'll wind up right soon," Mack said. "Come along."

They rode to the notch, and waited there in silence while the last red glow of a dying sun left the sky, and darkness spilled out across the desert. The junipers made a scattering of sharply pointed blots, the tang of sage was in the air, and there was a brittle sharpness to the night noises that rode the high, thin air.

Then there was the sound of boot heels on rock, the grinding of pumice on lava as the plug was lifted from its tight fit.

"I'll take him!" Mack whispered.

He drew his gun, and stood close to the notch as the huge slab of pumice moved forward until it was clear of the wall and the man carrying it was beside Mack. The Carne man had no warning, and he made no sound when the gun barrel came down upon his head. His arms broke free from around the pumice, and he sprawled limply forward.

Mack bound and gagged the man.

"Know him, Natty?" he asked.

"One of Kyle's men," the deputy said. "Reckon we're on the right track."

Mack had stepped into the V from which the pumice had been moved.

"Take a look at this, Natty," he said. "Don't it strike you they've chiseled this out some way?"

Natty felt along the edges of the notch, and moved on through the lava to the rim above the Cove.

"Looks like it. They must have put a charge of powder on this side. Reckon they wanted the side next to the desert to look plumb natural."

The lava flow paralleled the edge of the rim, a bare thirty feet between. Mack moved cautiously along the ridge which led to the Cove floor. It broke off gently from the rim, but was narrow, and both sides fell away sharply so that one false step would send a man pinwheeling through space to his death.

"Take it easy," Gordon called softly. "I ain't got my wings."

Mack had stopped, his ears catching an unusual sound. Gordon, too, had stopped.

"I thought I heard runnin' water," he said, "but we're too far from the creek to hear it."

"It ain't the creek, Natty," Mack said. "I'm thinking we've found out how they got Soogan's beef."

He moved on, and came presently to a saucerlike hollow in the ridge top. The gurgle of water was unmistakable now, and a moment later he sloshed into it.

"I'll be hanged!" Gordon breathed. He struck a match, its blaze shining across a pool of water. "They dug a hole through the lava wall, plugged it in the daytime with pumice, and took the plug out at night so's Soogan's cows would drift through for a drink. That it, Mack?"

"That's the way I'd call it. Come on."

"Look Mack." Natty stepped around the water and caught up with Mack. "You're missing something. How did the Carne boys keep Soogan's cows all this time?"

"That's what I aim to find out."

The ridge widened below the spring, and the evidence that a large number of cattle had come along it was unmistakable. Half an hour later Mack and Gordon had reached the floor of the Cove not far from Pioneer Creek. They stood in silence for a time, ears keening the wind for human sounds.

"You're still missing your ace," Gordon taunted.

"Which same makes you right happy," Mack murmured.

"No, it don't," Gordon said slowly. "Things have changed some in Axhandle while you was gone. It's my guess that if you stand trial, you'll find Kyle don't control the feeling like he did a week ago."

"Why?"

"Partly on account of the railroad agent bein' in town.

And then I reckon folks just kind of cotton to a gent who don't know when he's licked.''

"Let's mosey.''

Mack went on out of the boulders at the foot of the ridge and followed the edge of a grain field toward the haystack looming darkly before them.

"Darker'n a bull's insides at midnight,'' Gordon growled. "Just hit my big toe on a rock and drove it clean past my knee.''

Two wagons stood beside the haystack, and Mack thought of Dan Carne's load of hay and the water he had seen dribbling from it. That, more than anything else in this fantastic pattern of robbery and killing, had puzzled him. The answer had to be here.

He felt along the cliff until he was directly behind the haystack. Then the wall of the cliff broke sharply away from him.

"A cave!'' he murmured, his mind reaching out and gripping the possibilities that this fact held.

"Let's get back on top!'' Gordon shrilled.

"We'll have a look first,'' Mack said grimly. He knelt, cupped a match flame in his hand, held it close to the cave, and saw the marks of wheels and horses' hoofs. "A lot of wagons have gone in and out of here.''

"It's cold,'' Gordon said.

"A cave's always cold, even when it's warm outside.''

Mack went on, knowing that the important thing was yet to be discovered. He could see nothing in the pit-black interior of the cave, but he knew that somewhere ahead of him was the one missing part of the puzzle, the answer to the question Gordon had asked him.

Then the answer hit him in the face, something heavy and hard and cold that swung a little when he put his hand upon it.

"Natty,'' Mack said softly, "here's the beef.''

Mack struck a match, again cupping it in his hands and holding it away from him as he looked at the carcass. And it was in that instant that a gun bloomed ahead of him, the bullet laying open a gash along the back of his hand!

CHAPTER 19

Smoke of a Man's .45

The sound of the gun was cannon-loud in the narrow confines of the cave. Mack, acting instinctively, jumped around the beef and drew gun, and fell flat as his feet went out from under him. He lay there for a moment, utterly surprised by what had happened. Then he laid a hand palm down on the cave floor, and amazement for an instant stunned him. It was ice.

Another gun had taken up the fight. Behind him Natty Gordon cried out in sudden pain, and began shooting frantically. Mack slid forward, bullets making a whining sound around him, the gun thunder caught and thrown back in a series of prolonged echoes. They could not hear him, and Gordon was keeping their attention.

There was total blackness, with foot-long tongues of flame stabbing it briefly. Sudden silence then, and Mack held his position, body flat against the sheet of ice. He had come almost opposite the killers but he had no way of knowing if a frozen carcass hung between his position and theirs.

For the moment Natty Gordon had stopped firing. Then he opened up again, spreading his bullets, patiently searching the blackness for his target, the last slug coming uncomfortably close to where Mack lay.

There was no sound from the Carnes or Kyle or whoever it was that had fired, and Mack began to feel the chill of the cave. This had to be brought to a finish soon, and he had to make them give away their position. He drew a cartridge from his belt and tossed it against the wall of the cave about ten feet in front of where his enemies had been when they had fired last.

The cartridge clattered and bounced against the ice, a strange sound after the roar of guns.

"What's that?" Pete Carne's whiskey tenor cried out involuntarily.

Mack cut loose then. They were not more then twenty feet from him, and he was certain his first bullet got Pete. The man with him might have moved, and Mack was giving away his own position by firing. He emptied his gun, and slid another ten feet into the cave, pausing to thumb new loads into the cylinder.

"You got me in the leg!" Pete Carne burst out. "I'm bleedin' to death! Get a light and fix my leg!"

Still Mack made no move. He lay listening, wondering about the other man, and not knowing until Pete cried out again.

"I think yuh killed Dan. Get a light and fix my leg!"

"Throw your gun away," Mack said, and moved again.

Mack heard the gun sliding along the ice. Then Pete struck a match and held it alongside his pain-twisted face.

"There's a lantern over there," he said.

Mack kept him covered while he found the lantern and lighted it.

"Natty, you all right?" he called.

"Not quite!" Gordon shouted. "They got me in the left arm. Ain't bad. Who yuh got up there?"

"Dan's dead," Mack answered. "Got him in the side and the slug angled up into his heart. Pete thinks he's bleeding to death."

"Let him die," Natty Gordon said coldly.

Pete began to curse. "Yuh can't do that!"

"There's some things I aim to know," Mack said, "and you'll talk before I worry about that leg."

"What yuh want to know?"

"What were you doing back here at night?"

"Puttin' Hinton's hogs away."

"Who killed Jimmy?"

"Kyle done it. We caught Hinton inside the cove spyin' on us. Kyle left that gold button in Hinton's hand so's yuh'd think it was Soogan and maybe beef him."

"Metolius?"

"Dan and Kyle salivated him and Curly Usher."

"Why?"

"They got too hard to handle. Claimed they had a pardnership coming. Kyle had us pack Metolius over to Hinton's cabin, figuring you'd tell Soogan and the Tomahawk boys would figure you done it."

"Who shot at me in Hinton's cabin?"

"Kyle. We was keepin' an eye on the cabin thinkin' you'd show up. He'd have finished yuh if somebody hadn't come up and started shootin'."

"What happened to my letter from Hinton and the key?"

"Kyle's got 'em. That box in the bank had twenty-five thousand dollars in it and Kyle's goin' to need it because he's spread himself so thin he's about to lose his shirt. That's why he come in on this cow steal . . . Now you goin' to let me bleed to death in this cave?"

"I'll see what I can do," Mack said.

He stopped the bleeding with a tight bandage.

"Ain't as bad as he thought," he told Gordon. "He felt some blood on his leg and allowed he was bleeding to death for sure. Let me look at yours now."

Gordon's was a flesh wound just above the elbow, and was more painful than serious. When Mack had bound it, he held the lantern up and looked along the rows of frozen beef.

"There it is, Natty," he said with satisfaction. "You heard Pete say enough to hang Kyle ten times."

"A natural ice cave," Gordon said in awe. "Never been in one before. I reckon they brought the cattle in, butchered 'em, and hung 'em up. They'd keep here for a million years."

"Then they put 'em in a hayrack to haul them to town," Mack went on. "They'd throw in some chunks of ice and with the hay over them, they'd keep frozen a long time."

"That water you saw comin' out of the hay must have been the ice melting," Gordon said.

"Looks that way to me," Mack agreed. He stared at the beef hung from wooden racks extending in rows that continued farther than he could see. "Soogan will believe this when he sees it, I guess." He held his lantern to the side of the cave, and saw that it was solid ice. "They must have cut this out in the middle."

Gordon cleared his throat. "Cuss it, Mack," he blurted, "I sure have backed the wrong horse. I just wasn't smart enough to see through it the way they had the play rigged." He held out his hand, and when Mack took it, he added, "We'll tell Soogan a few things and then we'll nab Kyle. Now let's get out of here before I freeze."

Outside a man raised a cry.

"What's goin' on, Dan?"

Mack caught the faint figure of a man in the mouth of the cave, but only for a moment. As he reached for his gun, the figure faded into the night, and Mack, running after him, could not get his eyes on him again. A moment later he heard a running horse.

"We'll have trouble finding Kyle now, Natty," he said soberly.

Mack found two saddle horses hitched at the end of the haystack. He tied Pete Carne into the saddle of one, and he and Gordon mounted the other. Leading Pete's horse, they rode back to the notch. They tied the man Mack had knocked cold into the saddle of the horse Mack and Gordon had been riding, and mounting their own, took the trail for Axhandle. . . .

It was well past midnight when they rode into the town's dark Main Street, and locked a cell door on their prisoners.

"Get a Doc, Natty," Mack said. "Pete's leg needs looking after, and so does your arm."

"What you aiming to do?" asked the deputy.

"See if Kyle's home."

"That's my job, too," Gordon snapped.

"You're the law. I'm just a jigger with a personal problem I aim to work out with Kyle." Mack swung into the saddle again, rode around the block, and along the side street to Kyle's home.

There were no lights in the windows. Mack palmed his gun, found that the front door was unlocked, and slid in. He paused, listening, and then moved warily along the hall to Kyle's bedroom. It was empty. Mack lighted a lamp, and saw the evidence of flight. . . .

Mack had not realized how utterly weary he was until he reeled into bed. It was late afternoon when he awoke. Inky Blair was sitting beside him, his feet cocked up on the foot of the bed.

"Son," he said, "if you hadn't come around pretty soon, I was going after some of that ice to lay right on top of you."

Mack knuckled the sleep from his eyes, and grinned.

"Betty's got a meal fixed up for us," Inky went on. "Get up and whack off that sagebrush you've got on your face."

"I could stand a meal," Mack said. "Been eating kind of scanty lately."

While Mack shaved, Inky told him that the news had spread all over town, that Kyle and Terris had disappeared, that Gordon had taken a posse to the Cove, and had returned without finding any trace of Kyle.

"They found three hay hands in the Cove," Inky said, "but they didn't make any trouble. Neither did Kyle's men here in town. Seems like Kyle owed them some back wages, and they weren't thinking much of him. Fact is, Kyle was getting pretty shaky all around." Inky laughed. "And we had him pegged for a rich galoot. So did Soogan."

"Where is Soogan?"

"He's down at the Casino along with most of his outfit.

They went with Gordon this morning, and their eyes sure did bug out when they saw their beefs. They didn't find many hides. Seems that there was a hole just to the right of where you went into the cave, sort of a fissure that goes halfway to China. The Carnes tossed the hides and offal into that, figuring the hides were evidence they didn't want around."

Mack cleaned his gun, loaded it, and slid it into the casing.

"Tell Betty I'll be over in a minute," he said, and left the feed store.

Someone saw him, and raised a shout. They came out of the stores and business places, shaking his hand and slapping him on the back. This was not Lou Kyle's town now, Mack saw. Yet these were the same men who only a few days before had scraped and bowed in front of Kyle. Mack pushed his way through them, his face a granite mask, and went into the Casino.

Natty Gordon was inside with Wade and the Tomahawk men.

"There he is, gents!" Gordon called jubilantly. "The jasper who whittled Lou Kyle down to a right small size."

Mack thought fleetingly of that time only a few days before when he and Inky had stood in this same saloon and listened to Kyle make his announcements. They were days that seemed months, and the smell of powdersmoke and blood was still in his nostrils.

He had bargained for a home and a community where he could settle down. He had bargained for Rosella's love. Those were the important things, and he had not achieved them.

"Hod dang it, Mack!" Soogan Wade blurted. "I sure do hate to take a licking, and I hate to say I've been wrong, but I've taken a licking and I'm sayin' now I've been a stubborn, boneheaded fool."

He held out his hand, and Mack took it, a quick grin breaking across his face.

"We all make mistakes, Soogan," he said.

Wade pulled a roll of bills from his pocket and handed them to Mack.

"Five hundred dollars was our deal, and there she is. I

don't know what good that frozen beef is goin' to be to me, but mebbe I can keep on selling it to the railroad. I won't be getting three prices like Lou was, though.''

Mack swung to face Queen, and when he spoke, his voice crackled across the space between them with the venomous quality of a snapping blacksnake.

''George, I'm remembering how you aimed to hang Jimmy Hinton and how you claimed me and Jimmy stole Soogan's beef. Likewise how you said it would be a pleasure to smoke me down. I reckon now is a good time to try.''

But Queen had no stomach for it. He looked at Wade, his eyes narrowed and hard, his great pride slowly leaving him.

''You're hard on a man, Mack,'' he said.

''Not as hard as you was on Jimmy. You've got a one-inch brain with room for only one notion at a time. You're no ramrod, mister, and you'll ruin Soogan if you hang on. Now you can draw or drag.''

Queen laid his gaze on Mack's face, a long, searching look that seemed to tell him what he wanted. He wheeled and went out, and presently the sound of a fast-running horse came to the men in the Casino.

''Looks like I need a ramrod,'' Soogan said. ''Want the job, Mack?''

''No,'' Mack said, and left the saloon.

CHAPTER 20

Lou Kyle Makes His Play

Quietly waiting for Mack, Betty was standing beside the table in her living room. He stood looking at her, feeling the sweetness that was in her, the loveliness, the gallant womanliness that asked nothing of life except to give to those who were worthy.

"About time you was showin' up," Dad Perrod said.

"Sure is," Inky agreed. "My stomach's been missing you most. I'm hungry."

There was little talk while they ate, and when they had finished, Mack sat slack in his chair, the long tension gone out of him for a moment. He felt like a man who had been in a high wind, and just now had come into the quiet.

"What are your plans, Mack?" Betty asked.

"None right now." He looked around the room, noting that Rosella's wedding dress was not in sight.

"I said you couldn't do your fighting alone," Betty said, "but I was wrong. We weren't of much help."

"You were a lot of help," Mack said quickly.

He looked at them—fat-cheeked Inky Blair, gnarled old Dad Perrod and Betty. He felt the close ties that bound them;

the wildness and the fury of the past week had made those ties and nothing that lay ahead could change them.

"It would have been everything if Jimmy could have been here," he said softly.

"He's happy," Betty said, "knowing how it worked out."

"Funny about Kyle," Perrod mused. "I didn't think he'd run like this."

"I'll bet he's around somewhere waiting to gun you, Mack," Inky said.

Mack shook his head. "I've got a hunch he lit out for Trumpet. Jake Singleton will hide him out."

"I never heard of a natural ice cave, Mack," Betty said. "What would cause a thing like that?"

"Jimmy was talking about it one time. He said some caves don't have cracks in the lava floor, so water doesn't leak out. The cold weather lasts a long time at this altitude, and the water that dribbles in freezes. Probably come from that spring we found."

"But it's hot in summer," Betty said.

"Not enough to overtake the cold air in winter. Jimmy said something about a lagging effect in the change of temperature." Mack stood up, and stared down at Betty, hating to go, but knowing there would be no real peace in this country until the job was done. "Thanks for the dinner, Betty," he said and went out quickly.

As Mack left the restaurant he saw the stage was standing in front of the hotel. In a few minutes it would roll out over the valley road toward Minter City, and go on to the Columbia. If he were done here, he thought, he would take that stage.

"Mack." It was Rosella coming along the boardwalk behind him. When he turned, she came on to him. "I'm glad you're all right, Mack. I was worried after you left Tomahawk the other night."

"I made out."

He looked at her, a tall girl, perfectly poised and sure of herself, still feeling this man was hers, that she had never really lost him. She was here, within reach of him, and she would not be marrying Lou Kyle. This thought rushed through his mind, and he was startled by it, but it brought him no pleasure. He had made his dreams about this girl, and they were gone.

"I heard that Jimmy Hinton left you a lot of money," she said.

"I don't have it. I guess Kyle got it out of the bank box."

"You'll get it back," she said confidently. "What will you do?"

"Build a hospital mebbe. Jimmy would like the notion."

"Don't be a fool," Rosella said sharply.

"I can't help being that," Mack murmured, and turning away, moved toward the stable.

"Mack!" Rosella ran after him, caught his arm, and brought him around to face her. "Don't you understand?" She held up her left hand. There was no ring on her third finger.

"Yes," he said slowly. "I understand."

This time when he walked away she did not come after him.

Inky Blair was standing in front of the stable.

"You and Rosella," he said heatedly. "You crazy, blind fool. Betty's sold out and she's taking the stage. You didn't even say goodby."

"I'm taking a ride to Trumpet," Mack said.

As he walked past Inky toward the stall that held his sorrel, he knew he had no sure knowledge that Kyle had gone to Trumpet. The caution that the last weeks had developed in him caused him to drop a hand to gun butt. He was thinking, too, that it was strange the hostler was not round.

For a moment Mack stood motionless, eyes stabbing the gloom of the barn, and seeing nothing that aroused his suspicion. Inky was standing in the archway, glowering at him. Mack grinned, told himself he was getting boogery, and turned into the stall holding his sorrel.

He heard Inky call out in terror. That cry saved his life. He whirled toward the archway, and as he made the turn, a great fist struck him a glancing blow along his head and sent him reeling.

Lou Kyle and Tash Terris had been in the next stall. Mack caught the blur of their faces as he stumbled into the runway and spilled into the litter. There was a flow of red lights before his eyes, and for what seemed an eternity he lay there, the power of movement gone from him.

A gunshot would bring the town running. Kyle did not want that, but there was Inky to dispose of as well as Mack. So for a moment he hesitated, his Colt half drawn from leather.

"Get Blair, Tash," he said, and drew his gun to cover Mack.

Inky did not carry a gun, but he came lumbering toward them, armed with nothing better than a pitchfork he had grabbed from the barn wall. Terris started for Inky, but to reach him, he had to step over Mack, and Mack brought his legs up in front of the big man and sent him into a hard fall.

Kyle had no choice then but to fire, the bullet lifting a geyser of dust within inches of where Mack's head had been.

Mack had brought himself to his knees, lifting gun as he came up, and for an instant did not know why Kyle had missed. He fired, and as Kyle began to fold, he saw the pitchfork on the ground. He knew then what had happened.

Mack came to his feet, and spun to face Terris just as the big man got up and charged him, the bright blade of a knife flashing in a huge hand. Mack fired twice, the second bullet catching Terris between the eyes and bringing him crashing again into the litter of the stable floor.

Kyle was not dead. He lay, one hand clutching his shirt front, his eyes shadowed by death.

"Got into too many things," he muttered. "Lost my head in a poker game in The Dalles. I might have pulled out if I could have married Rosella soon enough. I've got Hinton's money on me. I—I . . . ." His lips tightened as a spasm of pain swept over him. "I'll beat you to perdition, Jarvis. I aimed for Tash to snap your neck, but we didn't know Blair was in the barn. You've got the devil's own luck.''

Mack, standing over him, saw Lou Kyle die, a death that would bring peace to the Axhandle country.

Men poured into the stable then, Dad Perrod among them, and as they came Mack heard the thunder of the stage as it crossed the plank bridge. For the first time the realization came to Mack that Betty Grant was leaving town, that she was going out of his life. And with it was the full knowledge of what she meant to him.

"Thanks for heaving that pitchfork, Inky," Mack said, as he threw gear on his sorrel. "You saved my life, which ain't worth much and won't be if I don't catch that stage. Inky, get that dinero off Kyle, and Dad, pick this horse up."

He was in saddle then, and touching steel to his mount. He roared across the bridge, and a moment later came alongside the stage.

"Pull up!" he yelled.

The driver yanked on the lines, his face showing amazement.

"This a holdup?" he demanded.

"No. You're getting a passenger."

He stepped down, and took his seat in the stage beside Betty.

"Let her roll!" he called.

There were only the two of them in the stage. For a moment they looked at each other.

"Hello," Betty murmured then. "You going somewhere?"

"Are you?"

"To Minter City."

"A good town for a honeymoon," Mack said softly, "but we'll be back. We've got to help Inky Blair build a town."

He kissed her then, holding her hard against him, the soft sweetness of her lips building a fire that ran in a swift and torrid stream through him. This moment brought him to a place where he had never been before, a place where reality held everything that had ever been in his dreams. It was this for which he had fought; this for which he had lived. It was this for which he would go on living.

She lay inside his arm, her face upturned to his, and her smile was a glorious and beautiful thing which only Mack Jarvis would see.

"My dear," she whispered, "I thought you'd never know."

LAST COWMAN
OF LOST SQUAW VALLEY

CHAPTER 1

Man's Chore for a Button

Fate shuffled her cards and dealt fourteen-year-old Len Blanding the strangest heritage a button ever had. Len's grandfather—red-headed, two-gun Blaze Blanding—was the shootingest, fightingest, damndest hell-for-leather hombre who'd ever forked a bronc north of the Rio. But Blaze's life was cut short by a Union sharpshooter, and Blaze Blanding never came back to Texas.

Len's grandmother was a religious woman who hated the death and poverty of the frontier, and because she couldn't go back to her home in Georgia when the war was over, she moved to California and took her son Dan with her. There she died, and Dan drifted north to Oregon.

Dan Blanding was a quiet, soft-spoken man who somehow lived in a land of guns and trouble with neither a gun nor trouble. That is, until his death. Dan married a girl from The Dalles, and took up a homestead on the plateau south of the Columbia. Before the first year was out, his wife gave birth to Len. The next day she died. For fourteen years Dan was both father and mother to Len. He kept a house in Oxhead so Len could go to school. He raised cattle, made a little

money, and got along until the sheep came. It was then that
Dan met the trouble he'd always avoided.

There was a lot of his grandad in Len Blanding. He seemed
about half as big as a fourteen-year-old should be. He was
sandy-haired, blue-eyed, and had a face that looked as if
Mother Nature had run out of boys who needed freckles and
had tossed all she had left at Len.

He could ride any bronc that carried his old man's 2R
brand, and he could shoot the middle out of a four-bit piece
with his .30–30 as far as he could see it. All of which made
young Len gnash his teeth as he saw the sheep come into
Lost Squaw Valley and gradually take over the 2R range.

There was trouble in Lost Squaw Valley and the little town
of Oxhead, more trouble than just the sheep brought, and
more trouble than Len ever guessed. It was trouble that broke
wide open one winter day and spilled out its burden of death
for Dan Blanding.

On this particular afternoon Len had stopped after school
to play with Lottie Gillam's hound pup. It was dark when he
got home. His dad was pacing the kitchen floor, bearded face
twisted in a maniacal fury that was totally unlike Dan Blanding.

"I'll kill him," Dan Blanding said over and over. "Damn
his money-hungry soul, I'll kill him! I'll kill him!"

For a moment Len stood staring in amazement at his father.
Stood there while the cold wind blasted its way into the room
and drove away the warmth. But Dan Blanding didn't notice.
Len closed the door and leaned against it.

"What's wrong, Dad?" he said.

It was then that Dan saw the boy, and a trace of sanity
came back into his eyes. He sank heavily into a chair. "Everything, son," he said. "Everything. It wasn't enough for
the sheep to come. I didn't tell you, but last summer I had
to get a loan on the 2R from Rush Mellick. He said he'd
make it for six months and give me an extension. Now he
says he needs his dinero. I can't raise it, so he aims to close

us out. We'll lose everything, son—everything I've tried to build for you.''

"Don't matter about me," Len said hoarsely. "You figure Mellick's acting for the sheepmen?"

"That's the way it looks to me," the old man said. "Isn't like Mellick to want land."

"We shoulda fought them hellers when they first came."

"I guess we shoulda," Dan Blanding said miserably. "Didn't seem like there ever was a time when we was pressed enough to start slinging lead. Just gave a little here and a little there, and now we've got nothing but this house."

"Is this Mellick coyote the gent you was figuring on beefing, Dad?"

Dan drew a shaking hand over his face. "I—I was just talking, son. Just kinda excited. No use to kill a man, Len. It wouldn't help."

"Some low-down critters need killing," Len said stubbornly. "Like Mellick. He ain't fit to live."

"He'll have his time," the old man said. "Ain't our place to play God."

The strain of Blaze Blanding was strong in Len; so strong that now he looked disdainfully at his father. In that second his mind was made up. If his old man wasn't man enough to do this job, he'd do it himself. Mellick was going to die, and maybe his dying would teach the rest of the sheep crowd what they could expect when a cowman had been pushed too far.

Len started across the kitchen to the living room.

"Where you going, son?" Dan asked.

"Into my room," Len said carelessly. He didn't turn his head. He didn't want his father to see the grim purpose that had come into his face.

Len took his Winchester down from the pegs on the wall, tiptoed across the living room and let himself out through the front door. He buttoned his mackinaw around his neck, pulled the brim of his Stetson down over his eyes, and headed for Mellick's office.

He passed Lottie Gillam's house, saw her flaxen-topped head through the window and heard the yelp of her pup, but he didn't pause. A half hour before, he'd been a boy, playing with that same girl and her dog. Now he was a man setting out to do a man's job.

The spirit of Blaze Blanding walked with Len that night. Blaze had been only fifteen when he'd stood in the dusty street of a little Texas cowtown, and shot three bank robbers out of their saddles as fast as he could pull the trigger.

Blaze would have whispered in Len's ear, "You ain't killing a man tonight. You're stomping out a snake, a thieving, lying, crawling snake." Len didn't know much about his grandfather, but what Blaze would have said was somehow in Len's own mind.

CHAPTER 2

"A Rope Is Quicker!"

Two shots sounded from the center of town, crashing into the icy darkness and rolling down the deserted street. Len hardly heard them. He turned into Main Street and saw a light burning in Mellick's office. He crossed the street, opened the door and stepped inside. A lamp stood on the roll-top desk. In the chair beside it sat Mellick, head lowered on his chest as if he were asleep.

Len half raised his gun. It would be easy to let him have it. Too easy. Again Blaze Blanding might have whispered in Len's ear, "He's a skunk, son, but even a skunk deserves a fighting chance."

"Mellick." Len shivered. It might have been the cold he'd come in from. "Mellick." The money-lender didn't move. "Mellick!" Len raised his voice. "I've come to kill you. If you got a gun, start for it."

But still the man made no move.

It's a trick, Len thought, and shivered again. He eared back the hammer of his Winchester. Cautiously he crossed the room until he was only five feet from Rush Mellick. Then he stopped dead still. There were two holes in Mellick's shirt front over his heart; two holes from which blood had flowed to redden the cloth of his shirt.

Mellick was dead! Len remembered the shots he had heard. Slowly his hand moved forward and touched the man's face. It was still warm. One thought leaped into the boy's mind. His father had known what he'd aimed to do, and he'd got here first. Peaceful, mild Dan Blanding had killed the man who'd ruined him.

Quickly Len turned and ran out of the room, forgetting to close the door. Panic was in him now, wild, unreasoning panic. He didn't see the knot of men come out of the Domino Bar and head for Mellick's office. He only wanted to get away, to think over this astounding thing. He raced back across the street, down the sidewalk, past Lottie Gillam's house. Then he was in front of his own home, but he didn't go in.

His father was in the front room now, pacing back and forth. The rear of the house was dark. Len moved around to the kitchen door, and there he stood, out of the reach of the wind. For long minutes he didn't move, thinking of the grisly thing he'd seen, wondering now what would happen to his father.

A stray gust of icy wind struck around the corner of the building. Len felt the cold creep down his back. No use standing here. Maybe he could persuade his dad to get out of town. The street had been deserted. Maybe nobody had seen him.

Len went into the house and crossed the warm kitchen into the living room.

Dan Blanding looked up. "Where have you been, son?" he asked worriedly.

"Walking."

Dan looked at the rifle. "How come you was walking with your Winchester?"

Len had forgotten that the rifle was still in his hands. He leaned it against the wall. "Figured I might need it," he said slowly. "Dad, we haven't fought the sheep men. Why do you figure they want Mellick to close us out?"

"There's no quarter given between sheep and cattle men, son," the old man said. "We're the only cow outfit left north of the creek. With us gone, it'll be all sheep range. Then gradually they'll drift on across the creek, and take over the valley." He eyed the Winchester. "Len, I heard two shots a while ago."

The boy nodded. He didn't meet his father's eyes. Somehow he was disappointed. Of course his dad would have heard those shots if he'd fired them himself.

"Rush Mellick is dead," the kid said. He looked at his father then, saw the quick surprise in his face.

"Mellick dead?" the old man said.

"Two slugs in his brisket," Len said slowly. Why was his father acting so surprised? He opened his mouth to say that his dad had better slope out of town, but he didn't have time to get it out. There was the sound of hoofbeats outside, and then the stomp of booted heels across the front porch. The door was thrown open, and a half dozen men surged in.

Blanding turned quickly to face the intruders. "Get out," he shouted thickly. "No damned sheep herders' hirelings are welcome in my house."

"We ain't asking," the man in front sneered. "We came to get you."

They'd come to get Dan Blanding for Mellick's murder! Len knew that before they'd put it into words. His eyes searched their faces. The sheriff wasn't there. Suddenly he remembered that he'd looked out of the schoolhouse window and seen Sheriff Ashfork ride out of town that afternoon. He realized, in that second, that this crowd aimed to lynch Dan Blanding.

Len knew the men by sight. Ace Cottrell was in front, a vicious, cold-eyed killer. Behind him were Biff Randall, Slick Castle, Woody Lang, Trigger McKee, Slim Valley. They were gun-slung, callous hard-cases who'd drifted into Oxhead in the last year and had hired out to the sheepmen.

"What in hell do you want?" Dan shouted.

"You," Cottrell said harshly, "for Rush Mellick's killing."

"Me?" Dan stared at them. Slowly his eyes turned to Len.
He seemed to understand then. "All right," he said. "I'll
go to jail. Where's the sheriff?"

Cottrell laughed. "Ashfork ain't here, and we ain't waiting
for the law. There's a handy limb on that cottonwood in front
of the house. Git moving, Blanding. We'll show the beef-
eaters of Lost Squaw Valley they can't salivate an honest gent
like Rush Mellick."

Len grabbed up his rifle and thumbed back the hammer.
"Git out," he screamed. "You got the wrong man. I beefed
Mellick, but you ain't hanging me."

Cottrell stared at the boy. Then he laughed. "Listen at this
little pin-feathered rooster crow," he rasped. "It ain't you we
want, kid. It's your old man. Put that Winchester up before
you get hurt."

"I won't be the one getting hurt," Len cried. "Git out,
the passel of you." His trigger finger whitened. "Git out."

"Well now, button," Cottrell conceded, "that's a fair to
middling talking point you got in your hand. Maybe me and
the boys had better step outside and talk this over."

"Looks like we had," Randall agreed, with a sidewise
glance.

"Just keep going when you get outside," Len shrilled.
"Go on now, you—"

So intent was the kid on Ace Cottrell that he hadn't seen
Slim Valley edge away from the rest—not until Slim dove for
him. He whipped his rifle away from Cottrell, triggered a
wild shot, and went over backward as Valley grabbed his
legs. Then the Winchester was in Valley's hands, and Cottrell
and the rest were laughing.

"You got guts, kid," Cottrell boomed, "and we can't hang
a kid for trying. Just keep out of the way now, and we won't
hurt you."

Cottrell's gun came out and rammed into Dan Blanding's
back. "Git moving dry-gulcher. They say you never put up

a scrap in your life. This ain't the time to start." They had pinned a placard saying *Murderer* to Dan's shirt front.

Len threw himself on Cottrell, knotted hands flaying the gunman's back.

"Hey, git this mosquito offa me," Cottrell yelled.

Trigger McKee jerked Len up by the nape of the neck and held him in the air. "Just like a mangy pup trying to pull down one of Gillam's hounds," McKee snickered. Then he added in his tinny voice, "Want me to fix him, Ace?"

"Don't hurt the boy," Dan Blanding said, his tone high and fine. "I didn't kill Mellick, but you hellers ain't going to believe that. I won't make you no trouble. Just don't harm the boy."

"You won't make us no trouble, for a fact," Cottrell mimicked. He turned his gun toward Len. "Hold him up and stand away. No use being bothered by that scrawny wart. I'll fix him, Trigger."

"Hold on." Slim Valley had dropped Len's rifle. He stood crouched, fingers splayed over gun-butts. "You ain't hurting the boy, Ace. I figgered you was lower'n a crawling sidewinder, but I had you about ten pegs too high."

Cottrell stared at Valley, bewilderment in his china-hard eyes. Then he shrugged. "It ain't worth fighting over, Slim."

McKee cursed. "Pups grow into curly wolves, Slim. This kid ain't gonna forget tonight."

"You're damn right I ain't!" Len screamed. "If you're killing dad you better kill me or I'll get you. By hell, I'll kill every dirt son here."

"Drop him, Trigger," Valley spat the words.

McKee dropped Len by throwing him against the wall. Len fell like a half filled sack of wheat, and lay still. Dan Blanding twisted away from Cottrell's gun and leaped at McKee, but he never reached him. Biff Randall threw out a foot. Dan stumbled over it and sprawled on the floor. McKee brutally kicked him in the ribs.

"I oughtta beef you for what you did to the kid," Valley snarled at McKee.

"On your feet!" Cottrell prodded Dan's side with his toe.

He said over his shoulder to Valley, "You're getting mighty holy all of a sudden, Slim."

"I hired out to fight," Valley snarled, "not to slug kids. This hanging ain't to my liking, either. I say to hold him till Ashfork gets back and let him hang legal."

"We're taking no chances," Cottrell snapped. He had Dan on his feet now and was propelling him out of the room.

The rest filed out behind Cottrell and Dan and stopped underneath an old corral gate. Slick Castle threw a rope over the high cross-pole. Woody Lang fashioned a noose and dropped it around Dan's neck.

"Got anything to say, Blanding?" Cottrell asked.

"Just this," Dan answered slowly. "I didn't kill Rush Mellick. There's more evil in Oxhead than I knew. Someday it'll catch up with you. Men who live by the gun die by the gun. We couldn't stop the sheep, but honest folks can stop the work of coyotes like you."

"Cut off his blatting," Trigger McKee said in his tinny voice. "I came to a hanging, not to hear a preaching."

Cottrell jerked the rope, swung Dan high, and tied the rope to the corral fence. Then they all mounted their horses.

"Kick your way to hell, old-timer," Cottrell laughed. "The sheep are here and they're gonna pay. That right, boys?"

"You damn betcha," Woody Lang grunted. "Inside of six months the sheep will have Lost Squaw Valley, and we'll start collecting."

They moved down the street, all but Slim. He stood staring at Dan Blanding, and because he hated to see a man suffer, he drew his gun and shot him through the heart. Then he went into the house. Len was beginning to stir. Slim lifted him into a chair.

"You all right, son?"

Len rubbed his eyes, shook his head, and looked at Slim. "Did they—" He couldn't put into words what he knew was true.

Slim nodded. "I wouldn't go out front, button, and it ain't

safe for you to stay here. You better hike over to Gillams'. They'll take you in.''

Len shook his head. He couldn't say anything. He couldn't believe yet that his kindly dad was gone. Then he muttered, ''I'll get 'em. I'll get every one of them killers.''

''I'm not blaming you, younker. It's hell. But your dad salivated Mellick. Didn't give him a chance. Got him up close with a couple of .45 slugs.''

''You say .45 slugs?'' Something was beating at Len's brain. He'd supposed his dad had killed Mellick. Now he knew better. ''Dad didn't own a .45. All we had was our Winchester and a .38.''

''I wouldn't know about that.'' Slim shook his head. ''Cottrell said he saw your dad run out of Mellick's office, and we know he had reason to beef Mellick. Now you get over to Gillams'.''

Len struggled to his feet, swaying a little. ''You git out of here. You helped 'em. Go on, git out.''

Slim shrugged. ''Okay, son, if that's the way you feel,'' the man said. ''I did the best I could for you. Remember what I'm saying. You're not safe here by yourself.''

Slim Valley went out then. Len sat down and for a long time he didn't move. He had to go outside, but he couldn't bring himself to look at the thing he knew would be there. He knew, too, that Slim had been right. Cottrell or McKee or some of the others would kill him. They would have killed him before if it hadn't been for Slim Valley.

For some reason Len's mind went back to his grandfather. Dan had told him all the stories he knew of Blaze Blanding. It seemed to Len now that Blaze was talking to him.

''You've got to grow up, son. When you're a man come back and settle up, but you can't do it now. There ain't much a fourteen-year-old man can do, but a man can do a lot when he learns how to use a pair of sixes. You've got to be fast and sure and hard. Take life only when it's right. Never kill a man unless the world is better for his killing.''

It was then the boy made himself go out the front door. He saw it, that fearful, swaying thing that had been Dan

Blanding. He went down the walk, legs moving as stiffly as sticks, cut the rope and let the body down. He knelt beside it, laid a hand upon the cold face, and for the first time since Len Blanding could remember, tears flowed down his cheeks.

Dan Blanding had lived by faith, a faith instilled by his mother. Ironically enough, this man of peace had met his death at the hands of men who understood nothing but the talk of guns. Some of Dan Blanding's faith had come on down to his son. Now Len breathed a prayer. Not for his father. Dan Blanding had been a good man. Len prayed for himself. That he might be worthy of this father, and his father's father.

Then Len got up, went into the house and got a quilt. He came out, covered the body with it, and stood for a moment looking up at the chill, cloud-wrapped sky. There'd come a day when that same sky would see him riding back into Oxhead to repay this thing that had happened tonight.

CHAPTER 3

A Gunman Is Born

Len went back into the house. He put into his pocket all the shells he could find, dropped food into a sack and took the little money that was in the house. He didn't have much time. Somebody would find the thing in front of the house, and they'd try to make him live with the Gillams or Doc Freely or the preacher, and Len didn't aim to do anything of the sort.

The boy slipped out of the house, threw a saddle on the buckskin his father had ridden down from the 2R, tied the sack of grub on behind, slipped the Winchester into the boot, and swung up. He rode into a side street, kept off the main road until he was well out of town, and then turned toward the Red Dust Hills.

He could stay, Len thought as he turned his buckskin's nose into the wind. He could name the men who'd murdered his father, but he wouldn't be believed. They hung out in the Domino, Cottrell and his bunch. They'd swear they hadn't stepped outside all night, and Bat Singleton, who ran the Domino, would back them up.

Fred Ashfork would look at Len and say, "You're just a kid. I can't hold men on your say-so."

And that would be as far as justice would go. Len pulled the brim of his Stetson down over his eyes. There'd be justice, but it would be the quick, powdersmoke justice meted out by the son of the man who had suffered.

Dan Blanding's body was found an hour after Len had left town. He was buried the next day. Only a few of his friends were there. The Gillams, Doc Freely, the preacher, and some others. They looked all over town for Len, then gave up. If he'd left Oxhead, he wouldn't get far in this weather, they said, and he couldn't get out of the valley. The pass through the Tentrocks and the one along Lost Squaw Creek were filled with snow. He couldn't make it through either one, and they were the only ways out of the valley.

As the days passed, and nobody found Len, they gave him up. Lottie Gillam cried, and patted her hound pup, and remembered the afternoon Len had stopped on his way home from school to play with her and the dog.

Then the tears stopped. "He won't die," she told herself over and over again, her little face pale and tight. "He won't die. Some day he'll come back."

There were a number of things the folks of Lost Squaw Valley didn't know about Len Blanding. They didn't know how well this boy knew horseflesh, how much courage there was in his heart or the determination that was in him. Nor did they know that a man, let alone a boy, could make his way through the unmapped Red Dust Hills, and get out into the lower Battleground country, and stumble into a ranch-house, half starved, half frozen, but still alive.

For a week Ace Cottrell and his crowd hadn't ventured out of the Domino Bar. They didn't do much of anything but drink, and in their minds were Trigger McKee's words: "Pups grow into curly wolves."

"Why don't they find that damned kid?" Woody Lang brayed.

"He's under a snow-drift before now," Slim Valley said.

"How in hell do we know?" Cottrell thundered. "If it

wasn't for you I'd a fixed him so he'd never come back. Damn you, Slim, you ain't gonna live to see him come back.''

Cottrell jerked his gun out. Before Slim knew what the killer aimed to do, Cottrell shot him through the body twice.

''Now, damn you,'' Cottrell howled, ''roast in hell along with Blanding and his kid.''

Trigger McKee took a long drag on a bottle. He set it down, and his words were a prophecy. ''Only the kid ain't in hell. Some day he'll slope into town, and send us to hell. Let's git out of here when the snow's over.''

Cottrell fixed him with a long look. ''Not when we've got this good a thing. It's better'n being born in a mint. We'll stick. All of us.'' His cold eyes ranged over the four men who faced him. ''We'll make Lost Squaw Valley pay, and if and when that kid comes back, we'll give him the lead we shoulda given him a week ago.''

It was nine years and a spring before Len Blanding rode back through the Red Dust Hills and down into Lost Squaw Valley. There had been cattle, as Len remembered it, and bunch grass belly high. Now only sheep were here. But the town of Oxhead was the same. Len rode slowly down the wide main street, eyes straight ahead.

Almost nothing had changed. Bart Galtry's Mercantile, old Sim Cooney's saddlery, Doc Freely's dingy looking office, Bat Singleton's Domino Bar. Then Len was opposite the building where Rush Mellick had died. On the window was painted: JARED BLUESTONE, ATTORNEY, and as Len rode on, he wondered whether there was any business for a lawyer in Oxhead these days.

At the end of the business block, as Len turned his horse, he saw a sign in front of a white dwelling house. LOTTIE GILLAM, ROOMS AND BOARD. Lottie Gillam would be grown up now and making her own living. The story of that sign was plain to read. Lottie's father had been a cowman, and the day of the cowmen was long gone in Lost Squaw Valley.

Len turned into the livery stable. The hostler ambled up, a long-necked man with a huge Adam's apple that bobbed up and down as he talked. He took a look at the dust that gave a reddish tinge to both Len's black garb and his mount.

"Mister," he marveled, "looks like you came a long ways through the Red Dust Hills."

"Might be," Len conceded, and swung down.

The hostler eyed the horse. "Nobody ever goes through them Red Dust Hills, stranger, unless a posse drives him into 'em. In that case, you'll find Oxhead a mighty good place to rest up. Fred Ashfork's getting a mite old. He's the sheriff. Fred don't bother nobody that don't bother nobody else." He bit off a chew. "Right good looking animal you got, stranger."

Len stepped around the horse. "You're windy as hell, friend." Len stripped the black and dropped the saddle onto a peg. "Grain him double. I'm gonna want that bronc some of these days, and if he ain't in as good a shape as he is right now, I'll twist that skinny neck of yours and snap it off a little south of the middle."

The hostler swallowed, his Adam's apple bobbing around like a tumbleweed in the wind. He eyed Len a moment, took in his one hundred and seventy-five pounds, his six-feet-two of whiplash-muscled body, the sun and wind wrinkles that added to his twenty-three years, his great depth of chest and contrasting slimness of hip. His eyes paused on the pair of black-butted Colts, thonged down and carried low so that they rode close to the long-fingered hands. He swallowed and backed away.

"You betcha, mister," he mumbled. "I'll take good care of this animal . . . mighty good care."

Len swung on his heel and went into the street. There was no way of knowing how many of Cottrell's wolf pack still hung out in Oxhead, but according to riders who'd passed through Lost Squaw Valley, Cottrell was here, and it was reasonable to assume that some of the rest were.

There was little about this leggy, sun-darkened man to remind the old-timers in Oxhead of the knotty, freckle-faced boy who'd left town that fatal night nine years before. Nothing but the sandy hair and an arrow-shaped birthmark between his shoulder blades. There were hundreds of men with sandy hair, and the folks of Oxhead wouldn't be seeing the birthmark—if they even knew of it.

This was the way Len had planned it through the years. Now he was here to exact the tribute that Cottrell and his killers must pay.

There weren't many in Bat Singleton's Domino Bar. Just Bat, Slick Castle playing solitaire at a back table, and a trio of punchers drifting through. Singleton had seen Len ride past.

"Looks like we got a gunman in town," he'd called to Castle.

Castle laughed. "You're drinking too much of your own vinegar juice, Bat. Nobody in this burg would send for a gunman, but in case he is, I'll tend to him."

"Yeah," Singleton grunted, "but maybe you ain't as good as you think you are. I wish Ace was here."

"What you worried about?" Castle jeered.

Singleton didn't answer. He mopped off the bar, and kept his eyes on the window. Then he let out his breath sharply. "He's coming in, Slick."

Castle eased his gun in the leather. "Let him come," he said carelessly, and began to deal cards.

Len shouldered through the batwings and strode to the bar.

"What'll it be, stranger?" Singleton asked.

"Whiskey." Len looked at the three punchers and gulped his drink. Then he spotted Castle, covertly watching him out of the corner of his eye. The same Castle whom Len remembered, still wearing a fancy outfit; a flashy silk shirt, a chipmunk skin vest, a gold inlaid sixgun. A little older, that was all.

Len paid for his drink, and stared at Singleton, his blue eyes as hard as the barrel of one of his black-butted Colts. "I thought this was a saloon," he said suddenly.

Singleton went back a step, his flabby face taking on a greenish hue.

"Why, why," he mumbled, "it is. Anything wrong with your drink?"

"Plenty," Len brayed. "I don't drink with a skunk in the house. Pass over your greener, friend. You look like a back-shooting cousin to a skunk yourself."

Singleton retreated another step, all the time staring at this grim-faced, taciturn man. Suddenly he bent, picked up his scattergun and without a word passed it over the bar.

Len took the shotgun, brushed past the three punchers and strode to the table where Castle sat. The gunman shoved back his chair and got to this feet, fingers spread over gun-butt like the claws of an expectant hawk. This was trouble, all right; trouble coming closer three feet at a stride.

Len laid the scattergun on the table. For a second his eyes locked with Castle's, saw that the gunman didn't understand, and because of that, the man was afraid.

Then Len Blanding spoke. "Pups grow into curly wolves." That was all he said, so low that nobody but Slick Castle heard.

CHAPTER 4

The First Black Jack

For an instant there was silence in the big room. Of the six men there, four were frozen into immobility, waiting for this stark drama of death to unfold, while the other two waited for the first gunward movement.

There was a stir of sound over by the bar, and Len Blanding turned, his right-hand Colt seemingly leaping toward the lightning blur of his hand. The sound over there had been no more than the scrape of boot-leather on the puncheon floor. But in that instant, while Len's head was turned, Castle tried his play. High right hand flashed downward, touched the gun-butt, and started his draw.

Then Len whirled back. Twice his gun thundered, filling the saloon with its rolling echoes. Powdersmoke drifted upward. Castle's fingers fell lax and his half-drawn sixgun slipped back into its holster. He tottered on his toes, and died, knowing that Dan Blanding's words had come to pass: "Those who live by the gun shall die by the gun." Then Slick Castle's knees buckled and he sprawled on the floor motionless.

Len ejected two spent shells, shoved new loads into place

and holstered his gun. He drew Castle's fancy Colt from his holster, and slipped it into his waist band. He picked up Singleton's scattergun and strode out with no glance toward the four motionless men at the bar.

"I never saw anything like it," one of the punchers muttered. "Just the start of his draw and the result. Damned if that gent's human."

Bat Singleton, his face tight with unspoken fear, stared at the still moving flap doors, and felt that the puncher was right. This slim-bodied, taciturn man wasn't human. He was like an angel of death, and Singleton wished again that Ace Cottrell was in town.

Len walked rapidly down the street to Fred Ashfork's office in the front of the jail. Ashfork was reading a paper. He looked up as Len came in, and frowned. He was fatter than he had been nine years ago, and much older, his scraggly beard untrimmed and almost white.

"I just shot a man to death in the Domino Bar," Len said. "A skunk who used to call himself Slick Castle. Reckon he still goes by that handle."

Ashfork scratched his almost bald head. "Did you use all them guns you're toting?"

"One was enough," Blanding said curtly. "Two slugs in his brisket. There's three punchers in the Domino cutting the dust out of their throats. Reckon if you ask them, they'll tell you Castle drew first. I kinda figure the barkeep wouldn't give you the straight of it."

Ashfork lumbered to his feet. "I'll have a talk with 'em," he said. "I'm not gonna worry too much about anybody who guns it out with Castle, and is still on his feet. Howsomever, was I you, I'd be drifting on. Castle's got a couple of friends named Cottrell and McKee who are plumb lightning on the draw. They ain't gonna cotton to this business."

"I like it here," Len said shortly. "Reckon I'll stay and see what them two coyotes you mentioned aim to do about it."

Ashfork scratched his head again. "Be you the law, stranger? U.S. marshal or something?"

Len shook his head. "No. My trail crossed with Castle's a long time ago. I was just settling an old score."

The sheriff shrugged wearily. He looked like a very old man who felt his own futility. "Your scraps are your own business, stranger. There's a lot of hell in Lost Squaw Valley I don't just rightly understand. I reckon you won't be making things any worse, 'specially if you keep on salivating gents of Castle's caliber. I'll go have a look." He clapped his faded Stetson on his head and moved out of the office.

Len followed Ashfork a block, then turned down a side street to Lottie Gillam's house. A hound lay sleeping on the front porch. An old dog, Len guessed. Perhaps the same dog he had played with that winter afternoon so many years ago. At the other end of the porch, under the shade of a locust tree, an old man sat in a wheelchair, staring unseeingly down the street. It took a second glance for Len to recognize him. It was Rufe Gillam, Lottie's father. A shell of the man he had once been.

A young woman answered Len's knock on the door.

"You Lottie Gillam?" Len knew, even without asking. She was tall, and shapely. Her hair was no longer flaxen, but gold like ripe wheat, a color that matched the soft brownness of her eyes. She'd be twenty-one, Len was thinking, a woman grown.

He stood, looking down at her, and some of the hardness that the years had made in Len Blanding melted. There was no ring on her left hand, Len saw, and he was glad. Then he put the thought from him.

Lottie Gillam's full, red lips were smiling. "Yes, I'm Lottie Gillam," she said softly. "Can I do anything for you?"

Len jerked his head toward the sign. "It says room and board."

Lottie looked at the guns he carried. "You don't look like a man who needs room and board," she said. "You look like an arsenal that needs a gun rack and a lot of shells."

Len didn't smile. He held up the scattergun. "I drew the bartender's fangs, miss. And this—" he pointed to Castle's gold-plated Colt—"used to belong to a hard-case named Castle. He won't need it again."

"If that's the way it is, you're welcome," she said. "Come in. I'll show you the room."

It was a nice room with white curtains on the windows, a bed, a bureau, and a chair. It was the sort of room Len hadn't slept in since he had been a boy.

"It's a fancy room, ma'am," he said. "Too fancy for me, but I'll try to keep it kinda decent."

"We'll have supper in about an hour," Lottie smiled.

Len went back to the livery for his saddlebags. He shaved, washed the red dust from him and changed his shirt. Then he took six playing cards from one of the saddlebags and stood them up in a row along the top of his bureau. All were jacks of spades. One he turned face down, and laid the gold-plated Colt on top of it. His eyes turned back to the others.

"Five," Len muttered. "Ace Cottrell, Trigger McKee, Biff Randall, Woody Lang and Slim Valley." His memory ran back, clear and cold, to that grim scene etched so indelibly upon his mind. Of Slim Valley standing a little away from the rest, crouching, ready to draw against five gunhands to save the life of a freckle-faced kid.

The hope was strong in Len that he wouldn't find Valley in Lost Squaw Basin. He was the one man whom Len would hate to meet.

Blanding glanced at his watch. Lottie had said an hour, and the hour was up. He left the room and went downstairs to supper. Lottie introduced him to the other boarders. Frank Craig, bank teller; Link Doney, barber; and finally, Jared Bluestone, lawyer.

"I'm sorry, but I guess I forgot to ask you your name." Lottie turned to Len.

"Names," he said, "don't mean much. A man can change them like he can his hat. Reckon I won't use one."

"I see, you're a philosopher, Mr. No Name," Bluestone said sarcastically.

"You can call it that, friend," Len answered, and Bluestone's green eyes dropped before his gaze.

Lottie looked at Len uncertainly. "I guess we'll just call you Mr. No Name."

"It fits," Len nodded, "for the time being, anyway."

As Len ate, he studied the others. Craig and Doney he passed over as hard-working, honest men, but there was something evil about Bluestone. Handsome in his slick way, and carefully dressed, the lawyer was the sort of hombre Len disliked instinctively. Len didn't like the familiar, proprietary air the man used toward Lottie. He wondered what lay between them. The girl seemed cool enough, but there was no telling. . . .

That evening they sat on the front porch while the sun dipped from sight and the cool wind blew down from the Tentrocks. Lottie had waited on her father after the others had eaten. The old man was in bed now.

"Not much left of the old man." Bluestone looked at Len. "He used to be a prosperous cattleman, they tell me. Then the sheep came, and there was quite a scrap. The sheep outfit brought in some gunmen, and Rufe got a slug in the spine that paralyzed him. He's been that way ever since." The lawyer's eyes narrowed. "Gunmen are the scourge of this western country. A scurvy lot." His gaze dropped to the holstered Colts at Len's sides.

"Gunmen who hire out to sheepmen *would* be a scurvy lot," Blanding said in a level tone. "I reckon I'd put a shyster, who took sheep pay, in the same class."

Bluestone's angular face reddened. He bit his lip and looked away.

Craig suddenly got up and moved down the walk, his shoulders shaking in silent mirth.

CHAPTER 5

Hell Starts to Boil

It was dark by the time Lottie finished the dishes and came out to sit on the front porch.

Bluestone moved his chair close to hers. "You got no cause to work so hard, girl," he said. "It isn't right."

"I don't mind."

"All kinds of men come here," Bluestone went on. "You take them in and have them in your home. You never know what they are. . . ."

A silence then—a tight silence. There were four shadows on the porch. No light but the dull glow of Len's cigarette.

Then he said, his lips barely moving, "You don't like gunmen, Bluestone. I don't like lawyers. I'm going over to the Domino. I'll be there if you want to do anything about it."

Len got up and strode down the walk, and no one spoke until he had gone.

"You shouldn't have said that, Jared." Lottie's voice trembled. "He wouldn't harm me."

Link Doney stood up. "Think I'll hike over to the Domino," he said. "That ranahan didn't come to this town just for the ride. It's my hunch, Bluestone, that maybe he aims to put an end to the cussedness we got around here. Might be he'll get further than you or old Ashfork ever will.''

"I'm not the law," Bluestone said savagely. "Those Ghosts are mighty human and they're mighty tough.''

"You should know," the barber grunted, "since you do their collecting.''

"What else can I do?" Bluestone snapped. "Why doesn't Ashfork send for help?''

"I wouldn't know," Doney said. "But I do know I wouldn't suggest it, seeing what happened last fall to Matt Flanders.''

Doney left then, and when he was gone Bluestone took Lottie's hand. "Look," he said. "If you'd marry me, you wouldn't have to struggle for each nickel you make. You wouldn't have to put up with having a gunman in the house like this jayhoo. He doesn't even claim a name.''

"No, Jared." Lottie took her hand away. "I said I didn't mind.''

"But he's dangerous," the lawyer insisted. "He killed Slick Castle today.''

"Then he did the public a service." Lottie got up. "I'll have to go back to the kitchen. I have some pies to bake for tomorrow.''

"In that case," Bluestone said, "I'll follow Doney and your gun-slick boarder. Doney might be right. Maybe Mr. No Name has got something up his sleeve.''

The Domino was crowded when Jared Bluestone pushed through the batwings. The saloon was quiet. The sultry silence that comes to men when they feel the presence of Death. Then Bluestone saw what was happening.

Blanding was leaning over a poker table, a deck of cards spread face out before him. Opposite him sat Woody Lang, hands flat on the table top.

"I ain't taking that kind of talk from no big-mouthed pilgrim," Lang spat. "If there's five aces in that deck, I didn't put 'em there.''

"You're a damned liar," Blanding said. "You were dealing. There's five aces on the table, and four of 'em were in your hand. How in hell do you figure to lie out of that?''

The local gunman was on his feet, his head shoved forward. "You're gonna eat them words," he said slowly. "I'm gonna shove 'em down your throat with a chunk of lead.''

Lang's gun hand streaked for his Colt. Like Slick Castle, a few hours before, he got his .45 free of leather. Then Len's gun flamed in thunder so intense there were those in the crowd who claimed he'd fired but once. Lang bent double, grabbed the table and swayed.

Len came up to him. "Pups grow into curly wolves," he whispered.

Woody Lang's grip on the table top loosened. He pitched forward and died, the knowledge in his twisted brain that his fate had been decreed by his own evil past.

Len plucked Lang's gun from its holster, stuck it in his waist band and, as the crowd split before him, strode out into the night. As Len came into Lottie's house, he saw Bluestone in the kitchen. He was holding Lottie's hand, and talking rapidly. As Len moved on up the stairs, he saw the lawyer pull Lottie to him and kiss her.

Len closed the door of his room, dropped the second jack on its face and laid Lang's gun on top of it. He sat down in his chair beside the open window and cleaned his gun. He thought of what he had seen a few minutes before. It worried him.

Not that he could ever think of marrying Lottie. Nine years of drifting gave a man restless feet. There was this job to do, and then he'd go on. He had no roots in Lost Squaw Valley. Not now. Somewhere maybe, later, he'd settle down. When he was a free man. Free of this grim purpose that had been his for so long. But not yet. No, it was simply the fact that Lottie was fine and good, and Bluestone was bad.

A knock sounded on the door. "Come in," Len called. The door opened, and Jared Bluestone stepped into the room. Instinctively Len's hand dropped to his gun, then fell away.

Bluestone closed the door, smiled. "Reckon you didn't

expect to see me," he said slowly. "I just wanted to say that you did a fine job with Woody Lang tonight."

Len sat studying the man. The quick way he had of moving his hands reminded Len of a cat. That was it: a combination of a fox and a cat. That, to Blanding's way of thinking, was about as mean a critter as he could think of.

Bluestone took a cigar out of his pocket and began to chew on it. Suddenly he tucked it into one corner of his mouth and started to talk.

"I don't know why you're here, or who you are," he said, "but you've put two men out of the way since you've hit town. Both of them mighty tough hombres. It strikes me you're the man to do a good job for Oxhead."

He paused, his green eyes watching Len. Then: "For years this valley's had killings, robberies, extortions of one kind and another, and Fred Ashfork's done nothing. Then, about two years ago, all this stopped. The reason was that the owl-hooters, whoever they are, got together and organized what we call the Ghosts.

"Nobody knows who or what they are, but once a month everybody pays them tribute. Whoever don't gets his house burned, his sheep slaughtered . . . or maybe gets a chunk of lead. So folks pay, and the robberies and killings have stopped." Bluestone paused.

"I'm listening," Len said.

"That's about all. I'd make a guess that Lang and Castle were part of the organization. I don't know who else it would be unless Ace Cottrell is in it. He's not in town now, nor a couple more hard-cases that travel with him named McKee and Randall."

"Where do you fit in?" Len asked sharply. He sensed the fear Bluestone had of him.

CHAPTER 6

Trail of Ghosts

"Me?" Bluestone took his cigar out of his mouth. "I'm just the innocent bystander dragged in to do the dirty work. I collect the tribute once a month. Tomorrow's the day. I have to make a round of all the business places. They put the dinero in an envelope and sign their names. The sheepmen bring theirs in and leave it with Singleton in the Domino. After it gets dark, I ride out toward the Tentrocks, and somewhere along the trail a masked man relieves me of it. I've never got a lead on who it was. I thought once I recognized Cottrell's voice."

"There's such a thing as a trap," Blanding said. Then: "Why are you into this thing?"

"The answer to your first question is that Ashfork's tried a dozen times," the lawyer said. "Followed me; had men along the road; everything. But they're too slick. The Ghosts always seemed to know where the trap was. They'd jump me somewhere between the place where Ashfork had his men stationed. The other answer is Lottie. I think a lot of that girl. So much that I've been the tool for their dirty work. They've warned me several times that they'd grab her if I didn't follow orders.'' Bluestone made a gesture of futility. ''What else is there for me to do?''

''I wouldn't know,'' Len said, and fished the makings out of his pocket. ''If you want to know whether I'm sticking around, the answer is yes. Whether I run down your Ghosts or not, I can't say.''

''Tomorrow night I deliver the dinero,'' Bluestone said softly. ''I leave town at ten. Want to tag along?''

''I reckon not.'' Len yawned. ''I got other chores to do.''

''I thought so,'' Bluestone sneered. ''You got a chance to do the town a service, but you'd rather—''

Len was on his feet. ''Save it, shyster,'' he grated. ''Oxhead can solve its own problems. I've got my work, and that's what I'm aiming to do.''

Bluestone eyed him a second, his green eyes sparkling queerly. Then he went out and slammed the door.

Len stood staring after him, wondering what had been behind the man's palaver. Maybe he *should* go with Bluestone. Then the spirit of Blaze Blanding seemed to be in the room. ''No, son, you've only started to do your job. Don't let him or anybody in Oxhead get you off the track. The law here didn't keep your father alive, and you don't owe nothing to the law now.''

So Blanding went to sleep with his gunbelts hanging over the chair-back next to the head of his bed. The knowledge was in him that Cottrell and the others would come to town when they heard what had happened to Castle and Lang.

They'd guess the identity of this stranger with the lightning guns. They'd guess, and fear would be in them. . . .

After breakfast next morning Len waited until the others had gone and Lottie had fed her father and wheeled him back to his place on the front porch. Then he went into the kitchen.

''I'm kinda curious about something, ma'am,'' he said. ''Last night Bluestone was telling me about this Ghost bunch. Do you have to pay?''

She nodded soberly. ''At first I had to pay fifty dollars a month. I didn't want to pay it, but Jared said I'd better. Then, last summer, I got a letter saying I'd only have to pay ten a month. I don't know why.''

''What kind of a letter?''

''Just an envelope with a sheet of paper inside,'' the girl said. ''The letter was printed in pencil. Jared gets his instructions the same way.''

''Why doesn't he send for help?'' Blanding asked.

''He's afraid, just like the rest of us,'' Lottie said slowly. ''There was a newspaper editor named Matt Flanders. Last fall he began campaigning for Ashfork to do something. Flanders' paper building was dynamited . . . he was killed. I was going to write to the Governor, but Jared told me not to. He said I didn't know how ruthless these men were.''

''It's bad business,'' Len said soberly. He started to turn away when Lottie dropped her hand on his arm.

''I had hoped you had come to end all this,'' she said.

He shrugged. ''It seems to me this is the sheriff's business.''

Lottie's hand fell away. ''I guess it is. I—I guess I was hoping for too much. There's been evil in this valley for so long. It started over nine years ago, when I was a child. Sheep were beginning to force cattle off the range. The sheepmen imported gunmen. They lynched one of Dad's best friends—a man named Blanding. He had a boy I used to play with. Nobody knows what happened to him. He just disappeared.

''Folks said he died in the storm, but nobody ever found his body. Then that summer they shot Dad.''

Lottie was looking squarely at Len; he knew what she was going to say next.

''It seems like I've known you before,'' she said then.

''Bluestone called me a gunman.'' Len shrugged. ''It isn't likely our trails ever crossed.''

''But you aren't like these gunmen,'' she said gently.

Something stirred inside Len Blanding. Nobody had ever said anything like that to him before. There had been no kindness, no trust in the nine long friendless years. Now this woman was trusting him, telling him he was the kind of man who'd fight evil.

Strangely enough it was his father's words that came to his mind then. "Tain't our place to play God." And his grandfather would have said, "But God gave you a pair of fast, smooth hands. You still have a job to do."

Lottie was talking again. "I'd always believed that Len Blanding didn't die in the snow. I've hoped he would come back some day . . ."

"You liked that boy you played with?" A foolish question, Len knew, but nothing had ever been more important.

"Yes, I liked him," Lottie said softly.

"But, I reckon, if he came back now it would be too late. I mean, I figure you're getting set to marry this Bluestone hombre."

"I'll never marry Jared." Lottie looked at him squarely. "He's been good to me, and he's helped me, but I'll never marry him."

It came to him, all at once, that he wanted Lottie Gillam. He wanted to settle down. He wanted a home. He looked down at his hands, and had the feeling that the job he had yet to do and the job that must be done to free Oxhead were one and the same. . . .

Ashfork was sitting at his desk, staring at a pile of reward dodgers before him. He looked up as Len came in. "Well, stranger, Doc Freely's had a pile of undertaking business since you hit this burg."

"Looks like you're trying to find my mug." Len nodded at the papers lying on the desk.

"I ain't," Ashfork grunted. "And I ain't sorry. But I'd sure like to know who you are."

"Right now it ain't important who I am," Len said evenly. "What *is* important is why you let a bunch like these Ghosts milk hell out of people."

Ashfork tugged at his beard. "You want the job of running them down, stranger?"

"Maybe I do."

"Then look out of the window and you'll see three of the

toughest gun-slingers this country ever had,'' the lawman said. "I figure they're the Ghosts, but they're too damned slick for me to catch."

Len turned. Three men were riding down the middle of the street. Cottrell, Randall, McKee. Cottrell more arrogant than ever, his agate eyes flashing to one side of the street and then the other. Randall bearded, heavier. McKee's long-fingered hands were moving nervously.

"They look purty salty, all right," Len said dryly.

"Plenty salty. Pals of Castle and Lang. You'll have to smoke it out with them three or mosey on."

"I'll stay," Blanding said.

"Gunmen that came in here years ago." Ashfork leaned back in his chair. "Brought in by the sheepmen who, I reckon, have been plenty sorry since. Funny thing is that since these Ghosts been taking in the dinero, we don't have no killings or hold-ups except them that wouldn't pay. Cottrell spends most of his time on his horse ranch since then. Whoever runs them Ghosts is smart and slick. That ain't like Cottrell."

"Sounds a little more like Bluestone," Len suggested.

"Hell, no!" Ashfork shook his head. "Bluestone's all right. Got a good law business. He collects for 'em, but it's because he's afraid for that Gillam girl."

"But Bluestone knows the traps you've set," Len pointed out. "And they weren't organized until he hit town."

Ashfork reflected a minute. "Yeah, that's right. But it don't prove nothing. Why, folks around here are talking about running Bluestone for the legislature."

"Which don't prove nothing, neither," Blanding said. Then: "Say, there used to be a gunslick run around with Castle named Slim Valley. Know him?"

"He got plugged, years ago, in a brawl in the Domino," Ashfork said.

Len was remembering again that Valley had saved his life, and he was somehow glad that Slim Valley had gone.

"How many in this Ghost outfit?"

"Two or three," Ashfork answered. "Never more than

five. Of course, it's hard to say. On a lot of their dirty jobs we never saw anybody. Like the time they blew up Matt Flanders.''

Len began to roll a smoke. ''Sheriff, if you don't have no objections, I reckon I'll take some chips in this game. I'd like to sit here this afternoon and watch what goes on.''

''You're sure welcome,'' Ashfork said. ''I never had no hankering to swap lead with Cottrell. Maybe I'm too slow and ain't got the guts, or maybe I'm getting old. You're young and full of vinegar. If you're figuring on settling down, this would be the place. Election's this fall. If you clean this Ghost outfit up, the sheriff's job is yours. I've had enough.''

''We'll see,'' Len said. He didn't say so, but he knew now, since his talk with Lottie Gillam, that was exactly what he would like to do.

CHAPTER 7

One More Black Jack

Len went back to Lottie's house. Slim Valley was dead. Len turned another jack face down. Three still stood. Cottrell, Randall and McKee.

Last night he wouldn't have delayed, but it was different now. The hour of settlement could wait. He was on the side of the law. It wasn't just a personal matter. The law needed proof, and he aimed to get that proof.

Somewhere in this gun-rodded town was the Ghost leader, a shrewd, scheming man who wouldn't be easy to trap.

Len asked Lottie for two envelopes and two sheets of paper. One envelope he addressed to Bluestone. On the paper he slipped into it he had written:

> Two of the five have died. Tomorrow Lost Squaw Valley will be free. Where will you be?

The other Len addressed to Ace Cottrell. It said:

> There is always a day when thieves fall out. That day comes when the leader knows that the fools who take

his orders can be fooled. Do you know how much Bluestone collects?

Len mailed both letters in the early afternoon. Then he
went to Ashfork's office. It was almost six when he saw Cottrell go into the postoffice. When he came out he walked
slowly back to the Domino. Later Bluestone left his office
and got his mail. Presently he stepped back into the street
and walked briskly toward Lottie Gillam's house.

It was like Cottrell to be suspicious of Bluestone. He might
guess where that letter came from, but the seed would be
sown. Bluestone was different. Lang and Castle's death would
be bound to have an effect upon him. By this time the lawyer's nest would be well feathered. He wouldn't tarry in Oxhead if he thought the end of the Ghosts was near.

Supper was a silent meal that night. Doney and Craig did
the little talking that passed across the table. Bluestone hardly
lifted his eyes from his plate.

When the meal was finished Doney said, "This is the night
you're treasurer for the Ghosts, ain't it?"

Bluestone muttered something and went on to his room,
but Len caught him before he reached it. "You still want me
to ride with you tonight?"

The lawyer said over his shoulder, "Never mind. Like you
said, it's Ashfork's business." He went on into his room and
closed the door.

Len went back to the sheriff's office. Ashfork was still
there.

"Hang out in the Domino," Len said. "If you hear a gun
ruckus, come a high-tailing."

"What you figure's gonna happen?"

Len shrugged. "Nothing, maybe, but I think we may get
the blow-up tonight. If I was the boss of the Ghosts, I'd be
a mite worried seeing my outfit cut from five to three."

Dusk came, then darkness moved slowly across the valley.
Len had expected Bluestone to go to his office, but he didn't.
Blanding waited until nine-thirty, then walked into the Dom-
ino. Len didn't tarry. He took a drink, spotted Ashfork in

the back of the saloon, Cottrell and McKee not far from him. Biff Randall was nowhere in sight. Bluestone was at the bar talking with Bat Singleton.

The blow-up hadn't come. Disappointment was bitter within Len Blanding as he left the saloon. For an instant he was full in the light that cascaded from the barroom's windows, and in that instant gunflame ribboned the darkness from an alley across the street.

Len felt the tearing impact of lead in his left shoulder. He stumbled, jerked a gun with his right hand and plunged out of the lighted area. Once again the hidden gun barked. Len fired at the flash, and raced toward it, still firing. He heard a scream of mortal pain.

The dry-gulcher had had his one clear shot—and had failed. Even before Len had reached the alley, he guessed who the ambusher was. He struck a match and knelt beside the would-be killer. It was Randall.

The dry-gulcher stared up at Len's face in the flickering light. The match died, and Len struck another.

"You're sure a hell of a tough one to down," Randall breathed. He coughed thickly; blood bubbled to his lips. "We spotted you in Ashfork's office today. You're—you're Dan Blanding's kid, ain't you?"

Again the match flickered out. When Len struck the third one, Randall had died. Len hadn't time to tell him, but Randall had known, without being told . . .

Men had boiled out of the Domino and were crowding around Len. Ashfork was in front, a naked Colt in his hand. Somebody had a lantern, and in its red rays they recognized the dead man. Len searched faces. Neither Cottrell nor McKee were there. Nor Bluestone.

Ashfork saw the blood on Len's shirt front. "You're hit, man," he ejaculated. "Get Doc Freely, somebody."

Blanding allowed himself to be taken to Freely's office. The big job had still to be done, and his wound needed attention. He sat in the medico's chair while the wound was dressed. Then, when only Ashfork and the sawbones were there, the doc said, "I had an idea, from what's been happening, that you were Len Blanding."

Len stiffened. "How did you know?" he finally said.

"You were the first kid I brought into the world when I began practicing in the valley," the doc said. "You have that birthmark on your back."

"Dan Blanding's boy," Ashfork muttered. "Hell, I shoulda guessed. You came back to get—"

"Yeah," Len said somberly. "There's still two of 'em alive. I'm aiming to get 'em, and break this Ghost outfit. Get my horse, Ashfork. I aimed to trail Bluestone. I suppose he's gone now."

"You're in no condition to travel," Freely said.

"I'm traveling, anyhow." Len snapped. "Go on, Ashfork. Bring that black down to the Domino. If Cottrell and McKee are still there, I'll finish them right now."

The lawman moved as fast as his old legs would take him. Len picked up a bottle of booze the doc had on hand. He took a long swig. . . .

None of the men Len sought were in the Domino. One glance told him that. But Bat Singleton was behind the bar.

"Where's Cottrell and McKee?" Len snapped.

The saloonman looked at Len, then began to edge away. He'd already seen two men die.

"They left fifteen minutes ago," Singleton mumbled. He swallowed, and began to whine. "I couldn't keep 'em," he burbled. "I didn't know you wanted 'em."

"I hate a yellow cur," Blanding snarled. "And you're one. Where'd they go? If you're giving it to me wrong, I'll blast a hole in your fat belly big enough to shove that scattergun of yours through."

"Cottrell's ranch," Singleton managed. "I ain't lying."

"I'll find out," Len thundered. "If you are, I'll be back as sure as there ain't no water in hell."

Ashfork was waiting outside with the black gelding. Len mounted. "Where's Cottrell's ranch?" he asked the ancient lawman.

"The old Meador place," Ashfork said. "I'll go along."

"Better not, Sheriff. I'm not the law. I don't need proof. Hey—what in hell's this?"

A man reeled out of the blackness into the light from the saloon windows. It was Link Doney, the barber. He had one hand to his head; blood was dripping through his fingers.

"Bluestone," he muttered. "The heller's gone loco. He was taking Lottie with him. Telling her he'd beef the old man if she didn't. I tied into him and he slugged me."

The fear Len suddenly felt for the girl was a live, terrible thing. "Where would he take her?" he shouted at Ashfork.

"Hard to say," the sheriff snapped. "He'll head out of the valley. Down Squaw Creek, or up into the Tentrocks."

"Not yet," Doney whispered. He grabbed the tie-rail to hold himself up. "He'll need good horses. I heard him tell Lottie he was gonna grab some of Cottrell's Morgans."

"Get the Doc for Doney," Len shouted, "and round up a posse. I'm heading for Cottrell's."

"Wait!" Ashfork yelled. But Len Blanding didn't wait. He rolled his hooks and went thundering down the street.

Len knew the old Meador place, and the trail was as familiar to him as if he'd traveled it yesterday. His dad's 2R had lain just above it. As he raced through the night, the cool wind on his cheeks, he forgot his shoulder wound. He forgot everything except the horrible fact that Jared Bluestone had Lottie Gillam. *He* should have foreseen what Bluestone would do. His note had scared the lawyer into flight. Probably he'd been saving his loot for such a time as this. He'd think Cottrell and McKee were in town, and the horses would be easy to get. He wouldn't know that Cottrell and McKee had returned to the ranch. That was what made Blanding go cold inside. There was some decency to Jared Bluestone. There was none in either Ace Cottrell or Trigger McKee . . .

Chapter 8

Boothill Takes Over

Len Blanding hadn't prayed since the night he'd knelt beside the body of his father. Now he breathed a prayer that he might be in time. All these years he'd pictured Lottie in his dreams. He had found her all a man could wish for. That dream had been within the reach of his finger tips. Now . . .

Down the slope of Three Pines Canyon, across Indian Creek and up the long shoulder of Elbow Mountain, he rode. The jumpers fled by in a dark blur. Blood was oozing down Len's side from the shoulder wound. Every jump of his big black was a gamble with death, but these things were not in Len's mind. Only one thing mattered. He must not be too late. Once the outlaws had gone into the timbered stretches of the Tentrocks, it might be days before Ashfork's posse could find them.

Then Len was around the black shoulder of Crag Rock. Cottrell's ranch lay ahead. Len reined up his gelding. No light in the house, but a lantern gave its scanty gleam from where it sat beside a corral post. Len swung down and palmed a gun. He could see Lottie standing at the outer edge of the ring of light. Across from her, leaning weakly against the corral gate, Bluestone stood. Cottrell and McKee were facing the lawyer, their backs toward Len.

"I tell you it's all there," Bluestone was saying desperately. "I was bringing it out to you. Splitting three ways is better than six."

"It is, for a fact," Cottrell gloated. "We can thank that gun-fighter for that, whoever he is."

"You know who he is," McKee bawled. "For nine years we been expecting him to come back. Now he's here."

"He came back to Oxhead for nothing," Cottrell sneered at Bluestone. "He'll find the gal gone and you buzzard-meat." Cottrell drew his gun. "I've got a hunch you been robbing us."

"I tell you I aimed to leave this," Bluestone shrieked. "Don't kill me, man. Didn't I—"

"Shut up," Cottrell roared, then he fired.

Bluestone's head snapped back against a corral bar. For a second he stood there, one hand clawing at his heart, then his knees jackknifed, and he went down.

Len eased around the corral. He heard Cottrell say, "Let's ride. Toss that little saddle on Lady. The gal can ride her."

"The sooner we get out of here the better it suits me," Mckee mumbled.

"I'd like to swap a little lead with that Blanding gent," Cottrell said.

"Not me," McKee shook his head, and stooped to pick up the lantern. "Bat says he's the fastest thing he ever saw with a gun."

Len stepped away from the corral. "All right, bums!" he said.

McKee straightened, turned. Cottrell's gun was still in his hand. "They call me Ace," he said softly. "I got one in the hole now. You blast me and the girl gets it."

The dull ache of failure was in Len Blanding. Cottrell had called it right. He'd die, but so would Lottie.

"Well," Cottrell snarled, "what'll it be?"

There was nothing to do but play it out. Len saw that, but

he saw, too, that Lottie meant to do something. She was looking at him, her slim body tense.

"Looks like you've got that ace, Cottrell," Len said slowly. "But any way you figure it, you're cashing in."

"A big price, friend. You ain't smart—"

That was the second Lottie chose to leap backward into the darkness and fall. Cottrell's gun boomed, but Lottie kept on rolling until the night hid her. Len's gun was rising and bucking in his hand. Cottrell was down, but Len had wasted one too many bullets. McKee was firing.

A giant sickle cut Len's legs from under him. He was face down in the earth beside the corral. His job was almost done. Only McKee was left.

These jumbled thoughts were in his mind as he watched McKee's gun spewing fire. Again it roared. Dirt geysered in Len's face. Slowly he made his tired arm bring his Colt up. The hammer fell and the explosion almost knocked the gun from Len's limp fingers.

Everything was fading in front of his eyes, but there was no more gun thunder. Only the echoes that beat upon Len Blanding's brain as he slipped into a very dark place. . . .

There was no memory of the jolting ride back to Oxhead in Cottrell's buckboard. Nor of the fever-ridden days he tossed on the bed in his room in Lottie Gillam's house. It was the sixth day before he came to enough to know Lottie and feel her soft fingers pressing his hand. He dropped off again. The fever was broken. The next day things were normal.

Doc Freely looked him over. "He's all right," Freely said. "Let Doney come in and shave him. Then maybe he'll want to hear some things."

After the shave there was quite a crowd in the room. Lottie, Doc Freely, Sheriff Ashfork and Doney.

"You got a lot of sleeping to do, son," Freely said. "But I reckon you'd sleep better if you knew how things panned out. Go ahead, Fred. Tell him."

"Well, you did it," Ashfork rumbled. "That's about all to tell. Bluestone was dead when we got there. Cottrell and

McKee was dying. Sure was some shoot-out. Cottrell owned up to everything. Nine years ago he was the gent who killed Rush Mellick because Mellick was the head man of the gang, and Cottrell wanted to run it. He laid it onto your dad so the rest wouldn't know he did it. They pulled all the cussedness since that time until Bluestone came, and he talked 'em into this Ghost business.

"Seemed easier than all the hell they'd been doing, so they let Bluestone get 'em organized. Then you bobbed up. That's about all, son. Only when you're on your feet, you'll be wearing my deputy's star, and come election, you'll be wearing the big one."

"Now, clear out, everybody," Doc Freely grinned, "unless Lottie's got something to say."

They were gone then, and Lottie was sitting beside the head of Len's bed.

"You're really Len Blanding," Lottie said softly. "I sort of felt it all the time."

Len didn't say anything for a moment. He lay looking at her, and he thought he heard Blaze talking to him again. Blaze would have said, "You wound it all up, son. A woman makes a man soft, but it don't make no difference now. Go ahead and get soft."

"Lottie, will you turn them other three jacks down." When Lottie had done that and come back, he said, "That means the end of a chore I set myself out to do nine years ago. I can think of having a home now, and settling down. You reckon—maybe—you—"

It was harder to say than anything Len Blanding had ever tried to put his tongue to, but he didn't have to say it. Lottie helped him out.

"Maybe I could, Len," she whispered.

Len squeezed her hand uncommonly hard for a gent who'd been lying in bed for a week. As he lay looking at her, the bitterness that these years had brought went out of him. The drifting was done. He had roots here in Oxhead now, deep roots that would hold him.

HISTORICAL NOVELS
OF THE AMERICAN FRONTIERS

<u>DON WRIGHT</u>

☐	58991-2	THE CAPTIVES	$4.50
☐	58992-0		Canada $5.50
☐	58989-0	THE WOODSMAN	$3.95
☐	58990-4		Canada $4.95

<u>DOUGLAS C. JONES</u>

☐	58459-7	THE BAREFOOT BRIGADE	$4.50
☐	58460-0		Canada $5.50
☐	58457-0	ELKHORN TAVERN	$4.50
☐	58458-9		Canada $5.50
☐	58453-8	GONE THE DREAMS AND DANCING	$3.95
		(Winner of the Golden Spur Award)	
☐	58454-6		Canada $4.95
☐	58450-3	SEASON OF YELLOW LEAF	$3.95
☐	58451-1		Canada $4.95

<u>EARL MURRAY</u>

☐	58596-8	HIGH FREEDOM	$4.95
☐	58597-6		Canada 5.95

Buy them at your local bookstore or use this handy coupon:
Clip and mail this page with your order.

Publishers Book and Audio Mailing Service
P.O. Box 120159, Staten Island, NY 10312-0004

Please send me the book(s) I have checked above. I am enclosing $_____
(please add $1.25 for the first book, and $.25 for each additional book to
cover postage and handling. Send check or money order only — no CODs.)

Name _____

Address _____

City _____ State/Zip _____

Please allow six weeks for delivery. Prices subject to change without notice.

MORE
HISTORICAL NOVELS
OF THE AMERICAN FRONTIERS

BESTSELLING BOOKS FROM TOR

THE BEST IN SUSPENSE

☐ 50105-5   CITADEL RUN by Paul Bishop $4.95
  50106-3   Canada $5.95

☐ 54106-5   BLOOD OF EAGLES by Dean Ing $3.95
  54107-3   Canada $4.95

☐ 51066-6   PESTIS 18 by Sharon Webb $4.50
  51067-4   Canada $5.50

☐ 50616-2   THE SERAPHIM CODE by Robert A. Liston $3.95
  50617-0   Canada $4.95

☐ 51041-0   WILD NIGHT by L. J. Washburn $3.95
  51042-9   Canada $4.95

☐ 50413-5   WITHOUT HONOR by David Hagberg $4.95
  50414-3   Canada $5.95

☐ 50825-4   NO EXIT FROM BROOKLYN by Robert J. Randisi $3.95
  50826-2   Canada $4.95

☐ 50165-9   SPREE by Max Allan Collins $3.95
  50166-7   Canada $4.95

Buy them at your local bookstore or use this handy coupon:
Clip and mail this page with your order.

Publishers Book and Audio Mailing Service
P.O. Box 120159, Staten Island, NY 10312-0004

Please send me the book(s) I have checked above. I am enclosing $_____
(please add $1.25 for the first book, and $.25 for each additional book to
cover postage and handling. Send check or money order only — no CODs.)

Name _____

Address _____

City _____ State/Zip _____

Please allow six weeks for delivery. Prices subject to change without notice.